UNWANTED DREAMS

Elizabeth Parker

Copyrighted Material

Copyrighted © 2010 Elizabeth Parker

Title Page art from an original photograph by Elizabeth Parker

All rights reserved. No part of this publication may be reproduced or transmitted in any form by any means, electronic or mechanical, including photocopy, recording, or any information storage and retrieval system, without permission in writing from the publisher.

Unwanted Dreams is a work of fiction. Names, characters, places, and incidents are the product of the author's imagination. Any resemblance to actual persons, living or dead, or events, is entirely coincidental.

If you purchase this book without a cover, you should be aware that this book may have been stolen property and reported as "unsold and destroyed" to the publisher. In such case, neither the author nor the publisher has received any payment for this "stripped book."

Fifth Edition
ISBN 9781451559798

To order this book or any books written by Elizabeth Parker, or if you have any questions or comments, please visit us at www.elizabethparkerbooks.com

A portion of the proceeds from the sales of this book will be donated to an animal rescue group.

A special thank you to my husband for all of your support and motivation.

To my pups, who inspire me each and every day.

Lastly, thank you Mom for always being such an important part of my life.

PART I

FIRST COMES LOVE,
THEN COMES MARRIAGE...

Chapter 1

Fate is ultimately defined as the preconceived notion that our future has already been determined. Regardless of the precautionary steps we take to avoid misfortune, our lives cannot be altered, and what was meant to be will be, whether it is a chance meeting or being at the wrong place at the wrong time.

Sometimes our destiny is fruitful and welcomed. Other times, a series of catastrophic events that impinge upon one unsuspecting person could easily produce a domino effect, distressing the lives of strangers and distorting the future forever.

March 1990

They were the perfect couple—young, smart, good-looking, and well on their way to having the ideal life.

It hadn't always been that way. Actually, it had been quite the opposite. Alexandra, more commonly known as Alex, was always a shy girl. Though naturally beautiful, she lacked the confidence that typically accompanied beauty.

Her parents thought she'd never date, much less find someone as wonderful and personable as Jack.

Jack, on the other hand, was always outgoing, charming, and confident in his appearance, manners, and the way in which he spoke. He had a firm handshake and looked you straight in the eye upon first meeting you.

There's nothing worse than initially meeting someone only to find that he shakes hands like a dead fish or looks at the ceiling as he says hello. Alex's father had always preached that those were the type of people you had to watch out for. If they couldn't look you in the eye, they were more than likely hiding something.

Whether speaking about the weather, sports, or just making idle chitchat, Jack's singsong conversations always possessed a polished luster that made you want to stick around to talk a little more. The inflection of his words made it seem as though what he said was the most interesting thing said all day—perhaps all week.

Prior to getting together as a couple, Alexandra and Jack had frequented the local bars and dance clubs separately with their own friends, as most twenty-somethings do. It was here that they began taking some slight notice of each other—which consisted of lingering eye contact that eventually progressed to occasional hellos, but that was about the extent of their meaningful dialogue.

A few months after their initial encounter, it was actually Alex who made the first move in starting a conversation. They were both hanging out at the Seaside Manor—a high-end bar/restaurant known for its beautiful and stylish décor, mostly of elegant cherrywood or black lacquer. Every weekend night, a popular local band was chosen to play, ensuring a large crowd and an even larger profit.

Alex was about to leave when she noticed Jack leaning against the bar, ordering a drink from the bartender.

Feeling courageous, she walked over to him. As she got closer, she stalled, pretending to take notice of the framed abstract art positioned on the wall, each piece carefully placed in perfect proportion to the rest.

Recovering her nerve, she inched closer and extended her hand to introduce herself. She feared he would say something rude and turn her away, leaving her to stand there looking like a complete fool. To her surprise, he did the exact opposite.

If there was such a thing as sparks flying, followed by love at first sight, Alex believed she had just experienced them both within a matter of a few breathless seconds. He had mesmerized her with his good looks and intrigued her with his intelligence and perfect manners.

They stood at the corner of the bar, barely noticing the enormous crowd encompassing them or the blaring music that screamed as they spoke. When they finally did look at the time, they realized they'd been standing there for almost three hours. It was ten past midnight, and Alex had to get home.

In her heart, she wanted to stay and talk all night, but knew her parents would be worried sick. With a great deal of regret, she made it known that she had to go, but not before offering her phone number on the back of a napkin in hopes that Jack would call.

As she said goodnight, Alex surprised both Jack and herself when she swiftly leaned in for a good-night kiss that seemed to last forever. She pulled away almost as quickly and, as she ran to her car, realized she regretted the kiss—at least somewhat. She was certain that this newly-discovered forward nature of hers would deter Jack from ever calling.

When she got home, she went to her room and rested her head on the inviting, fluffy pillow. Though not the least bit drunk, she felt as if the room was spinning. She fell asleep, hoping upon hope that Jack would call as he'd promised, and dreamt about him for what seemed like the entire night.

Chapter 2

The morning sun was barely rising, and the fog seemed to lift, promising a beautiful spring day on the sandy shores of Long Island. Though the skies above illuminated the day with brilliance, the mood in the air was somber and dismal.

The police had no concrete leads. The killing seemed random, yet so perfectly staged. It was as if the killer had wanted this victim to be found or at least hadn't gone to any great lengths to try and conceal it.

The estimated time of death was around 1:00 a.m., and investigators had surmised that the victim must have known his assassin. There was no struggle, no contact—just a gunshot wound to the chest. Clean, simple, and effective. No witnesses had come forth claiming to see or even hear anything out of the ordinary. It was as though there hadn't been one person within earshot of this killing, which seemed almost impossible. The neighborhood was fully developed, and occupied houses stood only a few feet away.

No weapon had been found, just the fatal bullet that had entered the heart of the victim—a male, estimated to be twenty-eight years old, seemingly well-groomed and healthy, aside from the gaping hole in the middle of his body. He had nothing on his person that indicated who he was, where he was from, or why he'd been the target of a horrific shooting.

No one had yet been reported missing, but only about eight hours had passed since the murder. Someone would have to step forward, claiming this young man as their friend, son, brother, boyfriend, or co-worker; even an acquaintance would suffice.

Reporters swarmed the area like bees drawn to honey, as it wasn't a common thing for a murder to take place in such an affluent area. Police cars, emergency vehicles, and news vans with extended cameras saturated the crime scene as well as the adjoining blocks. Yellow caution tape blocked off any entrances to the area so that local bystanders wouldn't be subjected to the horror that had taken place only yards from where their children played ball in the park.

This upscale portion of Long Island was typically a good, safe area; the kind where you hope to raise your kids and, with any luck, eventually enjoy retirement. There was the occasional robbery or domestic violence reported, but nothing that ever stood out—and definitely nothing that warranted this level of news coverage. The Suffolk Police Department never had to answer a call from someone who had found a body hidden in a makeshift grave.

The police would be thoroughly questioned, and they knew they'd better come up with an answer sooner rather than later. The public was sure to go haywire within a few short hours. How could a possible local man be murdered in such a prestigious area? This wouldn't be tolerated. Not in this town. Locals began gathering closer to the crime scene, huddling together to see if any of their neighbors had acquired the inside scoop.

Once they made a positive ID on this unfortunate man, investigators would have more luck piecing together the clues and finishing the puzzle. The problem was that he had no identification on him—no license, no wallet, no identifying features to give this poor soul a proper name. All they had to go on were a few footprints and a somewhat old wrist watch.

Usually the dead can speak, only not in a language most people would understand. Often, there are subtle clues that paint a sad and grim story, helping to properly bury the victim and, with any luck, convict the appropriate suspect.

If the victim or suspect had no prior records, chances are there would be no fingerprints on file to match those found on the watch. From this point on, it was just a tedious, prolonged game of wait and see.

Chapter 3

At 8:00 a.m., the sun shone through the slightly opened window as the phone on Alex's nightstand rang. She had literally just woken up and was still trying to decipher whether she had dreamt up the whole fantasy the night before or had actually *met* the man of her dreams. As she answered the phone, she got the answer she needed and, more importantly, wanted.

"Good morning, sleepy head. Hope I didn't wake you. I'm also hoping you remember me from last night. It's Jack."

"Of course you didn't wake me," she lied. "I've been up for hours. Did you say your name was Jack? I remember speaking to a Dan, but, hmm, Jack doesn't sound familiar."

Now that he had officially called, she had to give him a healthy portion of her iniquitous teasing.

"Only kidding. I actually just hopped out of the shower and was about to go get some breakfast."

"Great! I knew you couldn't forget me. I *have* been told I am unforgettable. How about some company? I could be by your place within twenty minutes. I'm starved!"

"Um, sure. That'd be great." As she responded, she wondered how she'd possibly shower, find the perfect outfit, and be ready in twenty minutes. "Need directions?"

"Well, we discussed a lot of things. However, I don't think your address was among them. So, yea, may I have directions?"

She thought about sending him out of the way a bit, just to buy her more time, but she quickly decided against it as she was anxious to see him after only a few short hours of being apart.

After speaking with Jack and rushing around to get ready in time, Alex found that she actually had three entire minutes to herself. She needed it too, as she tried on close to five different outfits before settling on her favorite jeans and navy blue sweetheart sweater. She didn't want to appear overdressed, but definitely fashionable. This was, after all, their first official date.

They went to the local town diner for breakfast and got caught up in such deep conversation while indulging in a hearty feast of fluffy chocolate-chip pancakes, scrambled eggs, and crispy bacon, that they wound up staying for hours. After many coffee refills, they decided to extend the date a bit longer than anticipated and go to a matinee.

It didn't matter what movie was playing, as they had just wanted to spend more time together, consuming the overwhelming excitement that goes along with a successful first date. Unbeknownst to either of them, there would be many more dates after that.

During the weeks that followed, Jack found himself calling Alex early in the day to try and reserve time in the evenings to spend with her. On the weekends, he loved taking her out, whether it was going to dinner or spending the day at the beach. It didn't matter what they did. And to his pleasant surprise, she felt the exact same way.

They became closer with each passing day and barely went out solo with their respective friends anymore. They always included each other. It often felt as if they were moving too fast, but they learned a lot about each other in the short time they were together.

Family members were happy to see them enjoying each other's company, and when it came time for the holidays, they split the day between families: lunch at her parents', dinner at his, or vice versa.

As a matter of fact, after about eleven months of their inseparable courtship, Jack went to one of the most reputable jewelry stores and picked out a beautiful diamond ring. He knew her schedule day in and day out, so he strategically planned to arrive at her house one day when he knew Alex wouldn't be home.

He pulled up to the circular driveway, turned off the engine, and sat in the car, reciting the lines he had so diligently rehearsed over and over again. After about five full minutes, he checked his hair in the mirror one more time, got out of the car, straightened his clothes, and mustered the courage to walk up the driveway and ring the doorbell.

He almost hoped that no one would answer but was relieved when someone did. Alex's father was just the person he wanted to talk to, and after some meaningless chitchat, Jack worked up the courage to ask him the one question that almost every father wants to hear—providing they approve of the person asking it.

He was given the semi-threatening, half-joking speech of "if you ever hurt my daughter," etc., and then when it seemed that *some* fear had been instilled in Jack, Alex's father gave him the biggest hug and the long-awaited answer: "Welcome to the family." This was followed by a squeal of delight from Alex's mother and a nonchalant "right on bro" accompanied by a light punch on the arm from Alex's younger brother, Keith.

Chapter 4

Jack's proposal to Alex was nothing short of exemplary. He had arranged the perfect quixotic evening for them. A shiny black limousine picked them up to take them into Manhattan—the city that never sleeps. On the way in, they enjoyed a few cocktails from the fully stocked bar.

Upon arriving in the city, they enjoyed dinner at Gabriella's, an elegant Italian, private-style restaurant known to bring in a variety of famous clientele. A typical night of dining for two costs well above two hundred dollars, but the romantic and private candlelit ambience made it all worthwhile.

Toward the end of the meal, just before ordering the crème brûlée, Jack got down on one knee and surprised Alex with the life-altering question she had dreamt of for as long as she could remember.

He held open the elegant jewelry box containing an 18-karat white gold, cathedral diamond ring—the very kind she'd picked out in the jewelry store when they had only joked about getting married. "Alex, I can't imagine my life without you. Would you please do me the honor of becoming my wife?"

Her eyes filled with tears, but, mesmerized by the shimmer of the gorgeous ring, she couldn't bring herself to answer. The two entire seconds that it took Alex to answer Jack were the longest two seconds of his life. He suddenly felt nauseous, anxious, and all too worried that she would say no. Prior to this evening, he hadn't even *thought* of that possibility.

He was about to forget the whole thing and run through the restaurant doors when Alex screamed out, "Yes!" and threw her arms around him. He let out a deep sigh of relief and returned the hug, kissing his soon-to-be bride, relishing in the joyous moment.

The owner of the restaurant came over to personally congratulate them and offered dessert and a glass of champagne on the house, which they gladly accepted.

After finishing their scrumptious dessert and paying the exorbitant bill, they walked across the street to catch a Broadway show, both reveling in the happiness and excitement of the new life they were about to share.

Alex was beaming with pride and happiness, floating on the proverbial cloud nine, where she planned to stay for quite some time to come.

Chapter 5

Alex and Jack had a great time planning their wedding and made a point of keeping it a stress-free occasion. They didn't pay much attention to the minor details, focusing only on the absolute essentials.

While not traditional by any means, it was a wedding that many girls could only dream of. It was set to happen in July of 1991. Not being a fan of formalities, both Alex and Jack decided to have an informal, casual wedding set to take place on the sandy, private beach.

New York summers were known to be hot and humid, but the beach usually had a warm breeze flowing through, making the heat bearable, and sometimes the rain actually stayed away for special occasions. They hoped the rain would fully cooperate for this one but made sure tents were available just in case.

Alex, with her long, curly brown hair and glowing green eyes, made a beautiful bride. She wore a casual but elegant flowing white wedding dress. Everyone got a kick out of the fact that she wore faux-diamond-studded flip-flops on her wedding day, but somehow she managed to pull it off—looking as exquisite as ever.

Jack, of course, looked handsome and dapper in his pressed khaki pants and summery, short-sleeve dress shirt. He could wear anything and look like he had just stepped out of a magazine.

Everyone enjoyed themselves at the wedding and was happy to see the good-looking couple together. During the reception, Alex spent some time huddled in the corner giggling with friends, as she talked about her promising future with her new husband, where they would live and the type of house they'd buy.

Despite Jack's incredible personality, he didn't have many close friends. The ones he did have had been out of town for previously scheduled commitments, so they couldn't attend the wedding. His family, though a bit odd and eccentric, was more than happy to celebrate with them. A very friendly and polite bunch, they nonetheless had many qualities that sometimes separated them from the rest of the human race.

Jack's dad suffered from obsessive compulsive disorder. He wouldn't shake anyone's hand and, in most social situations, walked around with a face mask on so he wouldn't contract germs from anyone. He didn't wear the mask to the ceremony, and Jack and Alex felt slightly relieved.

Behind the confines of his own home, he was overly scrupulous in maintaining complete order so that not a trace of dirt could be found, not a magazine lay out of place, and items such as the remote control remained in the same location—in a straight line on the coffee table.

Not one ounce of laundry ever accumulated in his house. While growing up, Jack knew better than to leave him room in shambles or his laundry scattered around. God forbid Jack ever behaved like a typical teenager and left the dinner table without cleaning up his crumbs or wiping up his mess. All hell would break loose.

Jack's mother was a demure soul who could sometimes be found quietly crying alone in their bedroom. If ever caught crying, she'd claim she was just watching a sad television show, though the television never had a trace of even being turned on. She and her husband had a good relationship, on the surface anyway, despite their obvious differences in personality.

Jack had no siblings. He had never asked if this was his parents' choice or if there was some medical reason they hadn't continued to procreate. Not having a brother or sister was both a blessing and a curse. He enjoyed reaping the benefits of being an only child, such as getting any item that he wanted and being the sole apple of his parents' eyes, but he frequently wished he had a brother to confide in or a younger sister to look out for and tease on a daily basis.

Regardless of his parents' oddities, they managed to put them aside on this special day, have a great time, and welcome their new daughter-in-law into their life with loving arms.

Toward the end of the reception, Alex stood and asked everyone to raise their champagne glasses. "I'd like to make a toast. This is so exciting. I can't believe this is actually happening! I know those same exact words have been spoken by millions of girls all over the world, but a small part of me—OK, a big part of me—feels like I am the first and only person who is blessed enough to experience this.

"I keep looking down and expecting this to be one big dream, but the shimmer and glow of the beautiful ring resting upon my finger is a testament to the fact that this is real. I'm not only engaged, I'm actually married!

"Thank you all for sharing in our special day and for making our dreams a reality. I hope everyone can be as fortunate as we are."

Everyone clapped when the toast was over and the sound of clinking glasses filled the room. The last song of the evening played, and the temporary wooden dance floor positioned on the soft grains of sand filled with guests. Everyone participated in the last dance, even Jack's parents.

Afterwards, the guests packed up and headed toward their cars, wishing the couple luck and congratulations on their way out.

It had been a beautiful ceremony, and the best part was yet to come.

Chapter 6

Almost two years later, the Suffolk police still had no clues in the March 1990 murder. It was coming dangerously close to becoming a cold-case file. No one had claimed this John Doe.

A lot of promising leads came close, but when parents or next of kin came to identify the body, a positive ID could not be made. Two weeks after finding the deceased man, investigators felt a sense of great regret as they had to bury the body without discovering who he had been.

Unfortunately, they only had the clothes on his back, the wristwatch, the dirt in which he fell, and the large bushes that had partly shielded his body from the public as evidence. This in itself wasn't enough to reveal the ill-fated story of John Doe. The invisible rope tightly binding their hands was a devastating blow.

One of the most frustrating things for law enforcement to deal with is to give up and let the life and death of a victim fall by the wayside, without clues or justification. Even if there had just been a positive identification, at least there would've been a proper burial.

With this victim, they had nothing. His funeral consisted of lowering his coffin into a grave without any flowers or anyone to grieve or say a final prayer. His family and friends were sure to be somewhere out there looking for their loved one, dealing with the heartache of not knowing.

The killer, now classified as an UNSUB (unknown subject), had gotten away with it and lived to commit the same crime once again. Hopefully, he'd get caught on a technicality, maybe something careless like a parking ticket, and admit to everything.

This was, of course, a long shot, but one could only hope. There hadn't been any reported unsolved murders in a thirty-mile radius over the past fifteen months. It was possible this was a one-time act, committed with motive, or that the killer himself was dead. No one believed this, however. The popular consensus was that this person would strike again. It was just a matter of time.

The good news was that many serial killers are known to have some type of identifying signature—and this one was no exception. Though not discussed upon discovery of the body, that detail was revealed during the autopsy to the police. If this killer struck again, investigators would have a clue it was the same person. This killer had used a gun to kill his prey but left a very distinguishable knife wound on the victim's throat.

It was a seriously demented, very sinister, bone-chilling smiley face. The "smile" was the very one you'd find on a carved pumpkin that sits on a porch during Halloween.

Whoever did this was proud. He wasn't as concerned with getting caught as he was with leaving his mark. This last tidbit of information wasn't disclosed to the public in hopes that if the real murderer did call in to confess, he'd be able to give all of the descriptive, creepy details about his killing.

It has been said that once caught, a serial killer is more than happy to boast about the "work" accomplished. Most of them are a proud bunch, often with euphoric feelings of greatness or a "God complex," empowering them to take the lives of innocent, unsuspecting victims.

Keeping the details out of the media gives the killer an opportunity to reveal their sick story as only they want it to be heard. And investigators hoped that this suspect would soon find it necessary to speak up.

Chapter 7

They couldn't have asked for more perfect circumstances. Married only two magnificent months, Jack and Alex found a wonderful dream house only a few minutes from the beach.

It was a white Victorian with a large, wraparound porch—the perfect place to put a country-style double swing. There were four large bedrooms; three bathrooms; a parlor, living room, and dining room; and a dream-size kitchen with two newly purchased ovens—a must for Alex, who loved to cook.

There was also a room that could serve as a library or a workout room. Alex already had plans to make it suitable for both, as exercising and reading were two of Jack's and her favorite pastimes.

For Jack, there was an oversized, four-car garage. He was a bit of a car fanatic and truly believed that a spacious garage was a must for a man. He had a genuine knack for building things or fixing up the house and owned an abundance of tools to help get the job done with utmost efficiency.

The spacious yard spread out just over an acre and came fully equipped with a fairly new swing set, which fit precisely with their plan to start a family right away. There was plenty of room for an in-ground pool with tons of land to spare to start a garden or just add some pretty yard furniture. They could maybe even get a dog.

The inside was somewhat turnkey, but still required quite a bit of work. A couple of rooms needed to be spackled and painted, some of the banisters needed to be reset, and a few of the carpets could either use a good cleaning or, worse case, replacement.

Alex couldn't be happier. Jack was perfect in almost every way, and they were very much in love.

There was only one small thing that troubled her, but it was nothing to do with Jack himself—not really.

She'd been mildly disappointed at the wedding when she didn't get to meet any of Jack's friends, but understood they'd had prior commitments that couldn't be changed. That, in itself, didn't bother her.

What bothered her was that she and Jack had been together for almost eighteen months and she still hadn't met or even spoken to any of his friends. Come to think of it, Jack hadn't spoken to his friends since he and Alex had been together, not in her presence anyway.

It was only a slight issue, nothing to cause waves about. She thought about bringing it up that night after dinner. The possibility of even having a house-warming party would be a good reason to get everyone together.

Happy with her idea, she started planning what she could make her hubby for dinner. She'd gotten off work early from her job at the accounting firm, where she worked as a receptionist. Since she had some extra time, she wanted to cook something special.

She began preparing Jack's favorite—filet mignon with garlic mashed potatoes, creamed spinach, and stuffed mushrooms. A bit on the fattening side, but after savoring in the delicious spices, she was in the mood to devour it all without any guilt.

To Alex's pleasant surprise, Jack came home earlier than usual as well. He looked a bit caught off guard and borderline miserable as he walked in the front door and was greeted with a hug from Alex and the delectable aroma of her cooking.

His greeting wasn't quite rude, but the usual sparkle in his eyes had been replaced by a dark, empty stare.

"Why are you home?" he asked.

"Hi Jack; nice to see you too. Well, since you asked, the bosses had a golf outing and found it in their generous hearts to allow me to enjoy one of the last days of summer. I hope that doesn't interfere with your plans. Everything ok? I sort of just thought you'd be pleased to see me. Instead, you seem rather disappointed."

"I'm sorry, honey. I didn't mean it," Jack said, his expression softening. "Of course I'm happy to see you. It was a rough day. I had a few clients who were a bit on the obnoxious side, but you know us programmers. We can handle anyone. I'm fine now. Dinner smells great."

What he really wanted to say was that he felt so angry he could kill someone and that he had come home to cool down. He had expected to be alone and just have some downtime. This was one of those times when having a wife didn't work for him. He had to adjust to someone always being there to witness each of his emotions—good, bad, or indifferent. Today, his emotion teetered on the dangerously angry level.

A co-worker, Garrett, had gotten under his skin one too many times. The man had a particularly annoying habit of sucking the ice cubes after finishing the last sip of his soda. He'd stick his tongue to the roof of his mouth and make a loud sucking noise that infuriated Jack beyond belief. He repeated it over and over and over again until each ice cube was gone.

It made for a very long, frustrating day, especially if he had a super-sized cola from the local convenience store. It took Jack all of the willpower he could muster not to pour the cola on top of his co-worker's annoying little head.

And if that weren't enough to annoy Jack, Garrett had a second habit of coughing without covering his mouth, coupled with a loud, obnoxious sneeze that spread mucus spewing through the office.

Being raised to abhor germs, this was far too much for Jack to handle. He'd told his co-worker, Garrett, how much this annoyed him, yet Gar, as they called him, persisted.

Last on his list of annoyances was the fact that this person continuously sat there with a shit-eating grin, being overly loud when he spoke, chewing gum like a cow and popping bubbles like an ill-mannered school girl.

Gar never did an ounce of work, and his clients all secretly disliked him and, more often than not, described him as useless, dumb, or other similar insulting, but accurate, words. Jack was more than happy to add some additional words to describe his less-than-professional co-worker.

As a self-taught programmer, and a damn good one at that, Jack didn't feel he should have to deal day after day with a hideous, germ-spreading imbecile who probably didn't have one working brain cell in his head.

He didn't share any of these thoughts with Alex. He didn't want his newlywed, beautiful bride to know how crazy he felt at this precise moment in time. Unfortunately for her, she would begin to learn that on her own.

Dinner would be ready soon, and he had to admit that his stomach was rumbling and he was now looking forward to his hearty meal. He smiled at his pretty wife as he sat down, but not before giving her the kiss she'd expected when he'd originally walked through the door.

Dinner was delicious, as always. Alex was an amazing cook. He should've felt like the luckiest man alive to have a beautiful, smart, and funny wife who *also* knew how to cook.

"I've been thinking," said Alex.

"Hmm, what about?"

"Well, I've never met your friends, and we haven't seen your folks in a while. Why not have a house-warming party and invite them over? The weather's starting to cool down. What do ya think?"

"I think the idea is ridiculous and absurd, and how about I kill you for even bringing it up? What do *you* think?" That's what he wanted to say.

What he *managed* to say, after getting his temper in check, was, "Sure, let me know when you want to plan it, and I'll find out their schedules."

Alex's face lit up. "I'll put it all together and let you know. My parents are free most of the time. I'll call yours tomorrow, and then we can plan it. It'll be fun; I promise." Her mind wandered off, thinking of what to include on the menu and when would be the best time to have it.

She was absolutely beaming. This nagging little annoyance would soon go away, and her life could now resume being perfect.

After they finished their dinner and meticulously cleaned the entire kitchen (the apple didn't fall far from Jack's family tree), the two of them went upstairs and made passionate love. Alex felt connected to Jack on both an emotional and physical level.

She couldn't believe how fortunate she was. She forgot all about Jack's previously somber mood and remained focused on getting her dinner party together. She had the most wonderful husband, a beautiful house, and a marriage full of promise. Things just couldn't get any better.

Chapter 8

The next morning, Jack started his day feeling refreshed, like a brand new man. The night had been magical; the entire evening was divine. Nothing good ole Gar could do would set him off today.

As he approached his office, he found himself whistling a somewhat happy tune and laughed to himself. When was the last time he'd whistled? On second thought, had he *ever* whistled?

He opened the glass door, greeted the receptionist, and walked toward his office. As he turned the doorknob and almost made it fully inside without being noticed, he was interrupted.

He turned around to see Garrett standing there. In his loud, obnoxious, phlegm-spitting voice, he shouted, "*Hey, Buddy*! What happened to you yesterday? You left here so fast, we weren't sure what happened to you!"

"We?" Jack asked. "It was just you and me here, Gar. Everyone else was gone for the day. What '"we"' could you possibly be referring to?" Jack spoke between gritted teeth in such a low and angry voice that it was almost as if he were growling.

"Well, when you didn't come back, I called Scott and asked if he was with you. Ya know, I was worried about you. You never just leave here like that."

Had there not been a desk between them, Jack might've strangled him.

Scott owned the company. He decided who got a raise, who got promoted, who stayed and who went. He paid the rent on the building, and he made the rules.

One of those rules was that all employees were to stay at *least* until the end of their scheduled shift, unless they had a damn good reason. He wasn't going to be happy that Jack had left early.

Garrett knew full well that Jack had left without getting permission. It was Garrett's annoying habit of *living and breathing* that caused Jack to leave in the first place. How dare he call Scott? Furthermore, how dare he pretend to give a shit about Jack? He only wanted to get him in trouble. There was no mystery about that. He had one thing on his agenda and that was having Jack reprimanded in one way or another.

"So, Garrett, on top of every other rude, annoying, and disgusting habit that you have, you've decided to add snitching to your forever-growing list of pathetic, sociopathic tendencies?" Jack asked, becoming angrier by the second. "Thank you for unnecessarily getting Scott involved. I should've expected that from you. I'm fine. No need to worry about me. You're nothing but a stupid, useless lowlife, so bored and unhappy with your own life that you take solace in upsetting the applecart in the lives of others. Just one bit of advice: Worry about your own fucking self."

"But, Jack," Gar said innocently, "I was only checking to see if you were…"

"Fuck you, *Gar*. Talk to me again, and I swear I'll kill you. Consider yourself warned."

Jack's hands trembled as he slammed his office door behind him, and he thought his face must've been a frightening shade of blood red. He couldn't remember the last time he had become so angry; not even when Gar was sneezing all over the office.

He actually felt that if Garrett walked within five feet of him, he'd kill him instantly. Not only would he kill him, but he'd thoroughly enjoy it. He could actually feel his hands wrapping around his slinky little neck, gripping his flesh tighter and tighter until Garrett's face turned a weird shade of crimson red, and then eventually an obscure shade of blue.

He would smile as he sucked the light of life right out of him, the way Garrett sucks his stupid little ice cubes. He envisioned his slimy, germ-infested body slamming to the ground in one huge thud, and then it would all be over. No. more. *Gar*.

He got so caught up in the terrific fantasy that the phone must have rung four times before he snapped out of it. Of course, Garrett didn't answer it. Why would he? Useless piece of shit.

"Good morning; Jack speaking. How can I help you?" he answered in a surprisingly happy tone.

It turned out to be a client he had to meet a few towns away. They had a big project to work on, and it had to be done at the client's office.

As he walked out of the office, Jack screamed to Garrett, "Hey, *Gar*. I'm leaving the office. No need to go tell on me. I'm actually seeing a client. Mr. John Swazer. Check it out if you like, you stupid son of a bitch."

He felt full of life again. No need to play games and pretend to be all nicey-nice to Garrett. He'd pretended to like him and acted professionally for far too long. He was now able to speak freely and tell him what a useless jerk he was…and it felt good. Actually it felt a little bit more than good; it felt *amazing*.

Chapter 9

Three months had passed since the Garrett-killing fantasy, and no additional episodes had occurred. Garrett and Jack hadn't spoken since, unless it was absolutely necessary, and life was grand. He came home to his lovely wife and, as usual, dinner was on the table, but this time it was accompanied by candlelight, wine glasses, a bottle of wine, and a bottle of sparkling water.

"Wow, what's all this?"

"Can't a wife cook for her husband these days? I know you have had some rough days at the office and wanted you to come home to something nice."

"Thanks, honey. This really wasn't nec…"

"Jack! I'm *pregnant*!" She'd kept the news to herself all day and couldn't contain it anymore. She wanted to wait until they actually sat down to dinner and make sure that he had a glass of wine in his hand while she held a glass of sparkling water in hers. She *at least* wanted Jack to have taken off his coat, but she had to tell him immediately. She was glowing with happiness.

"It's official! I went to the doctor today, and I'm two and a half months pregnant." She didn't even wait to gauge his reaction; she just hugged him as tight as she could.

"Wow. I mean, really? That's great! I'm sorry; it's just that…I'm just at a loss for words. That's wonderful!"

Once he got over the initial shock, he gave her a big

There is one thing you should know though." She paused to sense his reaction and then playfully spilled the beans. "We're going to be quite busy, and might need a bigger car. I mean, two car seats *do* take up lot of room, and taking care of *two* babies isn't easy."

"Two? Twins! Are you serious? I mean, one is a lot of work, but two…"

"Jack, we'll be fine. We'll make it work. I promise. Aren't you excited?!"

The truth was that he was excited, as he really did want children; however, he just never imagined it would happen this quickly. He wasn't ready for it, as they had only been married a short time. For the moment, he wasn't feeling the genuine happiness that he had always imagined he would feel.

As they ate their dinner, Jack tried to mask a happy face but couldn't shrug the nagging feeling of such intense uncertainty. He didn't expect this stage in his life to present itself so soon. Alex, on the other hand, was confident and didn't show an ounce of fear, regret, or worry.

He decided to try and learn from her. It would work out. It would have to. He just hoped that he could eventually enjoy the same cheerfulness as his expectant wife.

Chapter 10

The next seven and a half months were exceptionally trying. Jack put in long hours at the office, and Alex got bigger and crankier each and every day.

They were never intimate anymore, and more often than not, Jack seemed aggravated with everyone and everything around him.

He snapped at Alex on more than one occasion. She even found herself arguing with Jack for no apparent reason. The due date was approaching soon, but it didn't seem soon enough.

On good days, they spoke about their plans for the future and had pleasant conversations about the baby.

Alex shopped when she could and brought home neutral baby outfits that would be appropriate for either a boy or a girl. Jack planned the date for Alex's baby shower with her mother.

The expectant parents were still amiably debating on whether Alex should continue working after the baby was born, or if she should work part time. Since Jack brought home a decent salary, they were leaning toward Alex quitting her job to take care of the two infants and perhaps hiring a nanny to help out during the first few months.

Those conversations took place on the good days. On the bad days, it seemed as though Jack was a complete stranger. If Alex brought up meeting his friends again, Jack completely lost it. She couldn't fathom what the big deal was and was getting frustrated.

She never felt Jack would lie to her about something, but his secrecy intensified her curiosity.

She dropped the topic for a while, as the housewarming party had been derailed by the news of her pregnancy, but it still weighed heavily in the back of her mind.

One evening when Jack came home from work, Alex couldn't help but bring it up one last time. Jack's response was downright creepy.

"Hey, Jack, how about we start planning our house-warming party?" she cheerfully suggested. "We never got around to it, and I'd still love to meet your friends. One last party before I give birth. I don't think this weekend is good, but how about the weekend after? I can start calling everyone and send the invites, and…"

"Well, honey, I have bad news for you," Jack interrupted. "We can't have the house-warming party. I'm no longer speaking to my friends, so please, let's drop it."

"All of them? Why? What happened? You never mentioned this to me. I don't underst…"

He waved his hands in the air as if to say, "Stop," and abruptly cut her off mid-stream. "You know what? Want to know what happened to my friends? I killed them. There. Does that make you happy? Just think of them as dead, and therefore, they can't possibly come to our party now, can they? Stop *asking* me about *my* friends. You obsess over the *dumbest* things. What bit of difference does it make? Enough already!"

"Jack, you sound crazy. You *killed* your friends? Who talks like that? What the hell is wrong with you?"

He ignored her trailing conversation and stomped over to the front door, pushing it open with what seemed like super-human strength so that the door opened and slammed heavily against the side shingles of the house. Without looking back, he stormed onto the front porch, stomped down the driveway, and simply kept on walking down the block, kicking sand and rocks along the way.

He'd been gone a little over an hour when he decided he had cooled down enough to make his way back. As he approached the driveway of their house, Jack saw Alex sitting on the porch in their double swing with her head cupped in her hands, picking imaginary lint off of her dress. As he got closer, she looked up but just stared through him as if he weren't there.

He got on his knees in front of her and put his head in her lap. "I'm sorry, baby. I didn't mean to blow up at you. I just haven't talked to my friends in a really long time, and I'm hurt that they didn't make it to the wedding. I'll call them soon. I promise, OK? There's just so much going on at work. It's been stressful. I'm so sorry. There's no reason to take it out on you."

He even managed to fake a long, drawn-out sob, and she believed him. They sat silently for what seemed like hours before finally making the decision to call it a night.

The next morning, no words were spoken between them, but an awkward, unspoken silence declared that the next few days were going to be rough.

Her baby shower was that Saturday. Despite all of the odd and hurtful things Jack had said, Alex was able to have a fabulous time. All of her friends, aunts, cousins, and even some people she really didn't know all too well were in attendance.

The gifts were incredible; she and Jack wouldn't have to buy anything for at least a year.

Within a few short weeks, Alex would be taking care of two babies. She couldn't wait, and at the same time, her anxiety increased. The only child she'd ever had any experience with was her younger brother, and she only had three years on him. She could hardly be considered a pro at parenting. She wondered if she even knew how to change a diaper.

Alex's mom sensed her daughter's apprehension and gave her a pep talk to help her through. She reasoned how it is every parent's fear that they may not be good enough and might fail at becoming a successful parent. She explained that while some things are learned by trial and error, for the most part, you learn which parenting technique works well for your family and you stick with them.

Although the pep talk helped to somewhat put her mind at ease, Alex still had some reservations. Regardless, she was looking forward to being a mom and had the utmost faith in Jack that he would be a magnificent father.

Chapter 11

July 18, 1992

Almost a year to the date after their wedding, Alex gave birth to lovely fraternal twin babies—a boy and a girl. Kevin, born first, was completely bald, while Amber already had a beautiful head of light brown hair. Both had blue eyes, but it would take time to determine whether they would remain that color.

Almost immediately after their birth, all the stress from the past nine months seemed to dissipate, leaving nothing but happiness circulating throughout the brightly lit hospital room.

Alex and Jack seemed so much in love, both with each other and the newborns. They were able to go home as a family within four days after Alex gave birth.

Once they got home, Alex and Jack fit perfectly into the role of Mommy and Daddy. They both seemed to be naturals. By the end of the first day, they were able to change diapers in record time, and making formula was a snap.

By the end of the first week, they had easily fallen into a manageable routine. Alex had been offered six weeks' maternity leave, but after weighing their options, she and Jack decided it would be best for her to quit her job and become a full-time housewife and mom.

This arrangement would benefit the entire family, as it gave Alex more time to bond with her children and still keep the house in some kind of order. Jack would be able to concentrate on his job, knowing his children were safe and in good hands.

Everything fell into place. They hadn't fought since that one outburst a few months ago, and it was, for the most part, long forgotten.

Days turned into weeks, and weeks into months, and before they knew it, the holidays were approaching. The entire family was in good spirits. Since this would be the twins' first Christmas, Alex spent most of her days shopping for the latest and greatest of toys for infants, unable to resist the clothing department, as well.

By the time Christmas rolled around, Jack and Alex were already discussing the possibility of having more children. The function of parenting was something they were both meant to perform, and it actually seemed to make them better people. Their children were well behaved, for the most part. They were not whiney as some children were, and they were already developing adorable, charming personalities.

During the weeks leading up to Christmas, both Alex and Jack went a little overboard with decorating. Some joked that they were a little bit out of their minds.

Inside the house, they had filled each room with Christmas decorations of one type or another, whether it was holiday towels for the bathroom or little snowmen knickknacks to sit atop the coffee table.

Holiday cards were strewn all over the house. They had positioned some on the mantle and hung others from a piece of yarn extending from one side of the living room to the other.

In the parlor, their enormous, real Christmas tree stood. Covered with tinsel, white lights, and ornaments—some new and some that Alex had collected throughout the years—it filled their home with the scent of pine.

Outside, Jack worked for almost a week hanging various colored lights that surrounded the entire house and strategically placing different types of figures on the front lawn. There was Santa with his reindeer and, of course, a sleigh; a full nativity set; and some cartoon characters from various popular Christmas movies.

On Christmas day, Alex had Jack's parents over, along with her brother and her own parents. She made homemade lasagna with all of the fixings for the main course. For dessert, she made her famous chocolate cake with dark chocolate filling and cream cheese icing. No one was able to resist this treat—not even those who claimed to be watching their weight.

Kevin and Amber were five months old, but even they seemed to be enjoying themselves. There were dozens upon dozens of presents under the tree for them, as they were getting spoiled by both sets of their loving grandparents and their adoring uncle. At this rate, they would never want for anything. Since there were no other grandchildren in the family thus far, Kevin and Amber would reap the benefits.

They tried to help the infants open the gifts, but, as predicted, the twins sort of fell asleep on the job. It was an amazing day, and the family had a wonderful time just being together. Some spouses marry into a family where they do not particularly care for their in-laws, but, fortunately for the both of them, everyone enjoyed each other's company.

Toward the end of the evening, they all made promises to have the Christmas celebration at Jack and Alex's house each and every year, inviting the same family members and, hopefully, adding some over the years.

They all hinted to Alex's brother that it was time he find someone and settle down. He pretended not to hear them and laughed as they all said their good-byes.

Chapter 12

The next few months were incredible. Jack was in a great mood and loved to be with the twins every chance he got. He called Alex about five times a day, just to make sure she and the kids were OK.

The children were both healthy, having not so much as a cough since the day they were born. Their growth pattern was right on schedule and they seemed to be fairly intelligent for their age, learning new things on a daily basis.

One day, when the babies were just approaching their eight month old mark, Alex wanted to surprise Jack at the office. She dressed Amber in a beautiful pink dress with little lace ribbon on the sleeves and tied her brown hair up in a tiny bow. She was definitely Daddy's girl—shy but with a noticeably charming personality, similar to her Dad.

She dressed Kevin in baby jeans and a blue polo shirt. He was such a happy baby, and Alex called him the apple of her eye. Though he was only eight months old, Alex lightheartedly swore that Kevin took pride in each outfit he wore.

As Alex pulled up to the office, the receptionist, Jill, ran to the door, ecstatic to see all of them. This was the first time she'd met the infants, and couldn't stop fussing over them. Jack heard the commotion and came to the front lobby, delighted to see his gorgeous wife and proud to show off his adorable children. They took part in a group hug, and he invited them back to his office.

As they walked together, they passed Steve along the way. "Steve, I'd like you meet my wonderful children," Jack said. "This is Amber and Kevin." Steve had already met Alex a few months prior.

"Hi, Alex. Nice to see you again," Steve said. Alex noticed he looked a little stressed, perhaps anxious. He wasn't rude, just a bit distant. "Your children are…beautiful." When he spoke, he held a prolonged, fixated stare as if he were looking through her, sort of like he was staring at a spot on the wall behind her.

Alex couldn't reason why, but chills ran throughout her entire body. It had never happened to her before in such a profound way—with such a powerful sense of uneasiness.

Goose bumps crawled up her arm, and she felt like someone was walking over her grave. She even stumbled a little and held onto Jack for a brief moment, just to regain her composure. If she'd stood there any longer, she was certain she'd faint. She didn't want anyone to notice, so she forged a smile the best she could, but was secretly happy to get away from Steve.

As they continued on to Jack's office, she forgot all about it and was just happy to spend some time with her husband. Jack welcomed it as well, as he noticed that since their birth, he ached to be with his children during the day. This was a welcomed surprise, and he embraced it for as long as he could.

He made sure not to introduce Garrett to his wife or kids, as he did not even consider him worthwhile, nor did he want to taint his family with any of Garrett's annoying habits. He almost felt like Garrett's personality and bad aura were catching, like the common flu. He shut the door to his office and played the role of Daddy for as long as his lunch hour would permit.

Chapter 13

The John Doe cold case still haunted the Suffolk police. Jim Delaney, a devout Irish Catholic and one of the best officers on the force, was especially troubled by it. He decided to sift through the evidence once more, looking a little more closely at the crime-scene photographs and bagged items taken from the area.

After spending the workday cooped up in the dreary office, dividing his time between staring at evidence and looking for answers on the depressing, grey walls, Jim wiped his eyes and was about to call it quits. Once again, he was defeated and felt like he had let this victim and his unknown family down.

He got up from his desk, picked up the evidence, and was about to put it back in the dusty file cabinets, probably never to be seen again. Most cops in this jurisdiction had moved onto newer cases, most of which would be solved in an expedient, efficient manner.

As he picked up the last of the bags, he noticed a particular item that he had looked at a hundred times before—a watch. Suddenly he had something similar to a flashback of where else he had seen it, only it was not in an evidence bag. It was strapped to the wrist of an actual living, breathing person.

Prior to becoming a police officer, Jim had tried his hand in the computer industry. He was extremely smart and knew more than most when it came to navigating around a computer. He'd been an excellent programmer, for a novice.

As it turned out, he became quite bored with the profession, which led him to joining the police academy. He did love the company for which he'd previously worked.

They were always fair, paid well, and gave a handsome bonus structure.

In addition, as each person achieved their tenth year, they received a gorgeous watch valued at approximately one thousand dollars. The company had been around for thirty years, but not many people Jim knew hit their ten-year mark during his era.

Most people had already moved on to better opportunities, retired, or had their positions terminated during that time. In fact, Jim only knew three people who had hit this milestone. A fourth man had also worked there for ten years but left the company just prior to Jim's start date. Jim had never met him, but he did know his name.

He turned the watch over, confirming his belief. On the inside of the watch, he read a short but sweet inscription: "Ten Years. Thank you."

This could mean one of three things. One: The victim wore this watch, and it fell off when he was shot. Two: This watch had belonged to a completely different person, unrelated to the crime. Three: The murderer wore this watch and didn't realize it fell off, or did but didn't have time to fetch it.

It wasn't a hot lead, but it was a lead nonetheless. Jim became ecstatic about his new discovery, wondering why no one had looked into this before. He figured someone had probably tried but simply hadn't known where to look. He sat back down and tried to recall the three people he knew at Symmetry.

He first thought of Joan Bellon. But she was a petite woman, and this was definitely a man's watch. It couldn't belong to her.

Next was Steve Johnson. A friendly man, Steve was somewhat quiet, kept to himself, and was fairly smart. He was a bit older and worked in the accounting department.

He definitely wasn't the victim, but did he have the ability to kill someone? Jim wasn't sure. Pleasant enough, Steve didn't seem like the killing type, though Jim had never really held a conversation with him that went far beyond sports and the weather.

Last on his list was Jack Rider. Jack had been Jim's friend while he worked at Symmetry. He was a stand-up guy, funny, and a great person to be around.

The only one who *could* have been the victim was the person Jim hadn't met, Michael Pardit. That meant that the only role Jack or Steve could have played, if any, was that of the suspect.

There was one issue that could make this finding a moot point as well. No fingerprints were found on the watch. A bit odd, but perhaps the owner needed help putting it on or had one of those gadgets sold on television to tighten the clasp. Some of those clasps could be tricky.

Jim decided that first thing tomorrow, he would go to Symmetry and find out Michael Pardit's whereabouts. If he was alive and well, or if he had died of known causes, that would mean that the watch didn't belong to the victim, leaving it to be the killer's—or, of course, just a missing watch.

Was it possible someone had simply lost their watch in the same spot as a brutal crime scene? Or could one of the watch recipients have actually been responsible for this hideous crime?

Chills ran down Jim's spine as he pondered the possibilities. Steve Johnson was a quiet man. He hadn't seen him in a while, but he couldn't picture him to be a cold-blooded killer. And as for Jack? Jack was his buddy back then. No. One of them must have simply lost their watch. Stranger things have happened.

Chapter 14

After a night of tossing and turning, Jim rolled out of bed bright and early the next day. He couldn't sleep a wink during the night, anxious to get started on his new lead.

He reasoned that it could be a dead end, but the more he thought about it, the more he felt this was the long-needed break in this case that had been haunting him, night after nightmare-filled night, for nearly two years. Like a possessive dog's fanatical obsession with a bone, Jim couldn't let this go.

He walked through the station doors with a light gait, feeling a new day was upon him. "Good morning, boss. I need to go check out a lead this morning."

Jim's boss, Captain Ackart, was always in the station earlier than most.

"Oh, yea? Which case is this for? Robbery on Main Street?"

"Not quite. I'll check it out and keep you posted. I don't want to raise any false hopes, and I'm not going to be putting myself in danger. I'll call you."

"Jim, wait!"

Jim grabbed a powdered doughnut as he walked out the front door. "Later, boss! I'll be in touch!"

As the door slammed, Captain Ackart cursed out loud, though no one was around to hear him. "Son of a *bitch*!" He knew full well that of all the men on the force, Jim was one of the best. He was just a little too headstrong for his own good. Jim knew very well that any time an officer was going to check out a lead, it was mandatory to have a partner with them.

Jim arrived at Symmetry a little after 7:00 a.m. Although the office didn't typically open before eight, he knew the loopholes, and the receptionist surely recognized and trusted Jim. She would let him in for sure.

As he tapped on the door, Jill put down her coffee cup and lifted her head from reading the morning paper. She pointed to her watch as she mouthed, "Sorry, we're closed."

She went back to reading the paper but heard the annoying tapping once more.

"Ugh. I'm *sorry*, but we're clos…Jim! Oh my god; I'm so sorry! Hang on a sec; gotta get the keys," he could hear her say through the tempered glass.

Opening the door, she embraced him with a welcoming hug. "Hey, Jim! I'm so sorry. I didn't know it was you. I haven't seen you in so long, I almost didn't recognize you! What brings you here?"

"Hey Jill. That's OK. Thanks for letting me in. I wasn't sure you'd still be here. How've you been? You look fantastic!"

"I'm doing great! Thanks for asking. Want some coffee?" She was genuinely happy to see him. Jill didn't have a malicious bone in her body. She'd had a pretty tough life, being on her own since her mother's death when Jill was only fifteen. Her father had taken off way before that, when Jill was only seven. He had found some younger woman and was never to be heard from again.

After Jill's mother died, she was left to fend for herself. She had no real family close to her, and those she did know were in no position to help her. She was an "old soul," as they say, but always had a friendly smile and would offer you whatever it was she had to offer. Although a bit of a gossip, she never harbored ill-feelings toward anyone and loved her job at Symmetry.

"Thanks, Jill. Coffee would be great, but I'll get it. Still in the same spot?"

In the corner of the room, the coffee pot stood in the same place it always had, surrounded by an assortment of bakery cookies Jill had brought in. Assorted crumbs layered the counter. Some things never change.

As he poured his coffee, Jim grabbed a cookie and offered Jill a refill as they got caught up. Jill gave him the inside scoop on who'd gotten married, who'd had kids, who'd been divorced, who was arguing with whom, etc. She had been working there for years and had no intention of leaving anytime in the near future.

Jill began to tell Jim a story about a guy she had been dating and how it hadn't worked out. The conversation then ventured toward a cruise she'd gone on over the summer. Jim didn't want to be rude so he let her continue on, hoping to be able to get to business soon.

Finally, she stopped talking long enough to ask Jim how he was and what was new in his life. He used this opportunity to try and find out some pertinent information.

"Jill, I just have a couple of questions I need to ask you. Were you working here when Michael Pardit was employed here?"

"Yeah, sure," Jill said, taking a sip of coffee. "Michael was a good guy. I was sorry to see him go. We got along really well. As a matter of fact, he always brought me bagels on Fridays. I loved working with him. It was so sad what happened to him, but you know what they say: 'Only the good die young.'"

"What'd he die of?"

"He was diagnosed with pancreatic cancer and died within six months. Nothing the doctors could do. It was unfortunate too, because he'd just quit smoking a few months before. I guess it was just too late. He left behind a wife and three kids. The funeral was devastating. So many people loved him."

"Hmm, I'm so sorry to hear that, Jill." There were two more possibilities. He was getting closer. He felt a little guilty about wanting to move on to the next topic while Jill was pouring her heart out, but he did have a job to do. People's lives could still be in jeopardy if there was a killer on the loose.

"How about Steve Johnson?"

"In accounting? Yeah, sure. He's still here. I'm convinced he'll never leave. Too set in his ways. He comes in at exactly 8:30 a.m. Never a minute late. And never does he leave a minute after 5:30 p.m. Remember how tight he kept his schedule? He in some kind of trouble?"

"No, no. Nothing like that. I just have a few questions to ask him."

It was getting closer to 8:30 a.m., but not close enough. Five minutes seemed like three hours. Jim actually had butterflies in his stomach. He'd told Captain Ackart he wasn't in any danger, but now that he'd had time to think about it, was that entirely true? Steve had never showed violent tendencies. Jim thought he would be fine.

"How about Jack? I'd love to see him. Where's he hiding out these days?"

Jill laughed. "He's here. Same old Jack. I still can't believe he's married with children now. I heard that he and Gar got into an argument though, a few months back. There's been a bit of tension flowing through these thin walls, but yeah, Jack's here. Sometimes he's here early, sometimes really early. Guess today he's going to be on time. Never late though a day in his life. Not unless he had a really good reason."

Jill looked past Jim out the window. "There's Steve now. I can see his car pulling in the parking lot."

Jim turned to look. "Steve's still driving that thing? I can't believe it's been eight years since I've seen him."

Steve parked his white Buick in the same spot he always used since Jim had known him. He was sort of a frumpy fellow, weighing well over two hundred and fifty pounds and reaching maybe five foot nine, with shoes on.

His posture was that of someone who had been carrying a heavy bundle in his arms, and while not considered jovial by any means, Steve still possessed the same friendly face, although he now sported a limp in his left leg. Jack wondered if that was something new or if he'd had that for a while. It didn't matter in the long run, but noticing new things was what Jim did for a living.

As Steve he walked in, he exclaimed, "Jim! Long time no see! What brings you here this morning? I know you didn't miss us, so it must be our delicious coffee," he joked, giving Jim a firm handshake hello and a pat on the arm.

"Hey, Steve. Certainly has been a long time. How've you been?" Staring down at Steve's ten-year token watch, Jim really second guessed himself about why he was there. Steve and Jack were not murderers, and they obviously were not the victim. The watch most likely belonged to Jack, as he was the only potential owner left who had yet to arrive.

He thought about opening the door and just making his way out of there. The watch was just a watch. No hot lead associated with it. It was turning into more of a waste of time.

Just as he was about to delve into Steve's personal life, the phone rang. As Jill answered it in her usual friendly voice, Jim noticed Jack wasn't in yet. It was 8:45. Steve and Jim got through some rudimentary small talk to catch up, and then Steve slipped through the doorway and headed toward his office, excusing himself to make a phone call.

"Oh, no!" Jill cried. "When did this happen? Priscilla, I can't believe this. I'm so sorry. I don't know what to say."

An uneasy feeling came over Jim as Jill finished the call. As she put the phone back on the cradle, she just stared into space and then looked up at him. She paused and tried to control the obvious tremble in her voice, but it was of no use.

In the most monotone of voices, Jill managed to deliver the unfathomable news. "That was Garrett's sister, Priscilla. She got a call this morning that Garrett's been killed." She said it more like a question than a statement.

She looked down and pressed her lips together. Trying to keep her composure, she continued. "He went out for a jog early this morning. He was supposed to stop by his sister's afterward to drive her to work."

She started really crying, her words becoming barely audible. "He didn't make it. They found his body a little over an hour ago. Someone murdered him this morning." In a whisper now, she said, "Garrett's *dead*." She repeated this last part almost as though trying to convince herself that he was really gone.

She ran into the ladies room and tried to gain her composure. She wasn't particularly close to Garrett, but murdered? Who would murder him? He was annoying, sure, but he didn't really have any enemies. Thoughts of Jack and Gar arguing ran through her mind. He wouldn't, would he?

Jim couldn't believe his ears. Murdered? It was an incredible coincidence that he was here during all of this…but where the hell was Jack? It was now 9:00. As Jill returned to her desk, Jim had to ask her. "Jill, I'm sorry. I know this is hard on you, but by any chance, did Jack call in and say he'd be late?"

Between sniffles, she was able to come out of her trance long enough to answer him before slipping back into a dazed state. "You know, now that you mention it, no, he didn't call. Maybe the children are sick or something. I can't believe this." She was talking more to the air than to Jim now, shaking her head every few seconds and closing her eyes, almost appearing to be deep in prayer.

Chapter 15

Jim excused himself to walk outside and call the station. Jill needed some time to let this all soak in anyway. He wanted to see who was assigned to this case. At least this time, they knew the victim's name. It was now up to them to find the suspect.

At about 9:15 a.m., Jim noticed Jack walking into the office, so he made a rush to meet him at the front door. "Hey, Jack. Nice to see you!"

"Hey, Jim! What brings you to this neck of the woods? I think the last time we saw each other was at the mall a few Christmases ago. We were both walking around aimlessly, trying to figure out what the hell to buy! How've you been?" Jack asked as they walked inside together.

"Good morning, Jill," Jack said. "Sorry I'm late. Had some last minute things to take care of. You know how it is. How's everyone doing this morning?" He looked at Jill's eyes and saw they were bloodshot with tears still streaming down her face. "Jill, you OK? You look like you lost your best friend or something."

Jim interrupted him before he said anything else that might set Jill off crying again. "Jack," he said softly, "Garrett's sister called a little while ago. I'm afraid there's been some bad news. Garrett has been…murdered." As he said *murdered,* Jim swore that the sides of Jack's mouth perked up just enough to form a smile. Could it be possible that Jack had *anything* to do with this?

"Wow. I'm, uh, shocked," Jack said. "Hmm. Oh well. I wish I could say I was sorry to hear that, but the truth of the matter is, I really just don't care. I think I was more upset when my pet goldfish went belly up. I never liked Garrett. As far as I'm concerned, he got what he deserved. It's nice to see you though, Jim. Let's catch up in a little while. I have some work to get started on."

He had started walking back toward his office when Jim interrupted. He recalled what Jill had said about Jack and Gar not being on the best of terms.

"Jack, can we talk for a second? I just happened to be here when Jill received the terrible news of Garrett's death. I understand you two had some sort of tiff a few months ago?"

Jim looked at Jack's wrist—no watch. Did Jack leave it at home? Did Michael Pardit lose his watch before he died of cancer? Jim felt as if he was on the treacherous drop of a rollercoaster ride, and his stomach did a heavy flip-flop. He should've called for backup after all.

"Jim, if you're asking me if I had a reason to kill Garrett, the answer is a most definite yes," Jack said. "I hated the guy. He was an annoying, malicious, idiotic slime bucket who never worked a day in his life, and as far as I'm concerned, he was useless every day of his pathetic existence. At least now, in death, he serves a purpose. The insects now have three square meals a day for at least a month—maybe more.

"If you're asking me if I actually killed Garrett, well, unfortunately, the answer is no. I can't take the credit for it, but I'd like to shake the guy's hand who did. Kudos to him. Gar probably pissed off the wrong guy one too many times and then *whack*; see ya!"

Jim was stunned. "Jack, as an officer of the law, I'm warning you that you are too damn close to becoming a possible suspect. As a friend, I'm suggesting that you tone down your hatred for the deceased. If you're innocent, no one will believe you with that attitude."

"Am I being arrested?"

"No. Not at the moment. But stay in town for the next few days. Let the police do their job, and you can go on living your life. No man deserves to be spoken about like that, especially before his body is even cold. I thought you had better morals than that."

Jim was more than pissed off at this point. He had neither love nor hatred for Garrett, but Jack's remarks were way past the point of distasteful. They were downright disgusting. "By the way, whatever happened to your Symmetry ten-year-anniversary watch?" he asked, pointing to Jack's wrist.

Jack looked truly perplexed. He couldn't remember where he had placed it. The last thing he recalled was removing the watch at work one day a few months back and putting it in his drawer, as it had been irritating his wrist. He didn't recall putting the watch back on.

He opened his desk drawer to see if it was there, but it was nowhere in sight. He wrapped his right hand around his left wrist as though this would trigger a memory of where his watch was and then shrugged it off.

"That's a good question. I took it off a few months ago and have no clue where it is. I haven't even thought about it since then. That watch is going on ten years old too in a few years. Guess that means I'm due for another one. The truth is I never really wore a watch prior to receiving one from here. It's 9:30 if you were looking for the time though."

Jim felt he should also go question Steve. No one had said anything about any altercations between Steve and Garrett, but he had to check it out.

Frustrated by Jack's lack of sensitivity, Jim called loudly enough so Steve could hear him from his office, "Hey, Steve. Got a minute?"

"Oh, are you still here?" Steve asked as Jim appeared in his doorway. "Thought you left. I've been on the phone all morning. As a matter of fact, I just hung up."

"Did you hear the news?" Jim asked.

Steve just sat there with a blank look and shook his head no.

"Well, there's no easy way to say this, Steve, so I'll just come right out with it. We received a call from Garrett's sister this morning. Garrett's been murdered."

Chapter 16

Alex was having a blast with the two infants, who rarely spent any time apart. The moment she took one twin away for a diaper changing or a bath, the other screamed in protest. There was some truth behind the theory of the strong bond between twins.

Alex realized early on that she would have to separate them periodically. Otherwise, they would grow up too dependent upon each other; it just wasn't healthy. She wanted them to have each other and even be the best of friends, but she was also a big believer in being independent.

Her new role of being a full-time housewife suited her just fine, and she grew to love it. She found working in an office rewarding only once a week—payday. Being a housewife rewarded her every second of every day. Watching her two children develop while they learned new things brought a smile to her face each and every time. She made sure to keep a baby book for each, recording almost every step they took.

Her digital camera stayed charged and ready to capture whatever it was they might be doing. While she was there to witness almost everything the twins did, Jack was not—and she didn't want him to miss a thing.

After vacuuming the entire first floor, she got the video camera ready to tape some good old-fashioned home movies. There were three full video tapes of the twins already, stacked in date order on the shelf nearest the television. She was expecting Jack's mid-morning phone call. Like clockwork, he called every day at 10:30. And today was no different.

"Good morning sunshine! How's my favorite wife today?"

"*Favorite*? You may want to rephrase that before I answer you!" she chided. "How are you? Anything new and exciting?"

"Well, I think we should get a sitter tonight and have a night on the town. It's been a while since we went to that restaurant you love. How's about 6:00 p.m.? What are the odds that your mom can clear her schedule and can watch the kids?"

"Sure, she probably can, but what's the occasion? You never call for a date night mid-week. What'd you do wrong?" she joked.

"Well, no occasion really. You're not going to believe this: Garrett's been murdered. That means I don't have to deal with his horseshit anymore. I thought that was enough reason for anyone to celebrate." He said this so callously, as if he were discussing the morning traffic.

There was dead silence, and then, "Jack, wait...what? He's been murdered? Seriously? And you want to celebrate? When did this happen? You aren't serious, are you?"

"As a heart attack. Whoops, guess that's a bad choice of words. But no, that's not the real reason I want to celebrate," he lied. "I just love the life and the lives we have created together." He paused, but Alex didn't respond.

"Garrett *was* killed though," he continued, "and I'm not upset about it, but...that's no reason to celebrate. Sorry for my joking at inopportune moments. You know me. I sometimes don't have that filter on my mouth that controls the deplorable words that escape it. I'll get better control on that.

"My old pal Jim, who now works on the police force, came visiting us today asking questions. Ironically, he wasn't there to investigate Garrett's death. He was working on another case from a few years ago. It seemed to be coincidental that Garrett expired on the same day."

"I'm sorry," Alex said. "With all due respect, you need to slow down. This is all too weird for me. I mean, I know you didn't have any love for this guy, but aren't you at least slightly upset? Do they know who did it? Does he have a family? Have they been notified? Doesn't this *bother* you at *all*? I can't imagine anyone being *happy* about someone's death!"

"Nah. If he annoyed me to the point of insanity, I'm sure he annoyed someone else just as much. I always knew it was just a matter of time. Oh, speaking of which, have you seen my Symmetry watch?"

"Random question, but no, I haven't seen it," Alex said. "What the hell does *that* have to do with anything? I hate it when you get like this, Jack."

"Nothing, I just don't know where I put it. I'll explain everything when I see you, OK? I promise." She could tell he was in a rush to get off of the phone. While she felt the need to get all the details of this bizarre killing and her husband's lax reaction to it, she figured the best thing would be to talk face-to-face over dinner.

"Well, OK. I'll call my parents now and see what I can do. Unless you hear otherwise, I'll be ready by six. I do want to hear everything. Please promise me at least that."

"I promise. I'm not crazy. Just dealt with Gar a little too much for my liking. If you'd worked with him every day, you'd understand my extreme hatred for the guy. You know me; I can get along fine with almost anyone. This guy though, I couldn't stand him from day one. I'll explain everything that I've been told when I see you."

Chapter 17

Steve answered all of Jim's questions with his notorious polite and quiet demeanor. He demonstrated no hatred or ill feelings toward Garrett and only spoke with the utmost respect for him. Jim had interviewed enough suspects and convicted enough criminals to know the telltale signs of a guilty suspect. He could easily notice any slight change in breathing, facial twitches, nervous hand gestures, or body shifting. Bad actors would sweat almost instantly the second they were questioned.

Steve spoke calmly and appeared undisturbed. Jim noticed, however, that he couldn't keep eye contact. He'd try and then quickly look away. He even tried to wipe his eye as if he had an imaginary piece of dust in there. But then he started to wipe the other eye in the same fashion.

He also had an interesting response when he received the news of Garrett's death. As Jim told him the news, Steve's answer was, "Oh, no. Not Garrett. How can someone just shoot another person? Who could do that to another human being?"

This was an expected or even an appropriate response from any innocent person upon receiving the news that someone was shot, except for one minor detail. No one knew how Garrett was killed. Jim hadn't disclosed this information to Steve. Garrett could have been stabbed, strangled, hit by a car—but Steve somehow assumed he was shot.

It could have been a lucky guess, but the hair on the back of Jim's neck stood on end. His gut revealed a completely different story, one in which he did not want to believe. He didn't have the legal right to formally question Steve or Jack until bringing them to the station, but he got the preliminaries in place. Homicide would have to do the formal questioning.

Years of being on the force had taught Jim to trust his intuition, sometimes more than the facts. Originally, he had suspected that *maybe* Jack had something to do with it due to his complete lack of respect for Garrett and his openly admitted hatred toward the guy. Now that he'd had some time to think about it, though, that was just Jack being himself.

Jack had never held anything back for as long as Jim had known him. He might have even been the most honest man Jim had ever met. He was usually charming enough without ever having to fake airs or graces.

Jim thanked both Jack and Steve for their time, asked them not to leave town until further notice, and gave Jill one last hug good-bye.

Once Jim left the building, Jack was able to concentrate and worked the rest of the day, making sure to console Jill every now and again. She was no stranger to difficult times, and he hated to see her so upset.

He went over to Steve's office, passing Gar's cubicle along the way. He stopped and tried to feel some sense of loss. Anything. But he couldn't help but feel just a bit too happy.

Steve's door was shut, so Jack pushed it open. As he did, he noticed Steve hastily hiding something in his lower desk drawer. Jack got a pretty good look though. If he didn't know any better, it looked like a magazine of bullets. "Steve?"

"Don't you knock? What the hell is *wrong* with you?"

"Sorry, man. I wasn't thinking," Jack said, trying to register what he just saw. He thought about what other, normal, sensitive people would say. "Terrible thing that happened to Garrett, wasn't it?" he managed.

Why would Steve have bullets at work? Why would Steve have any bullets at all, and *why* were Steve's hands shaking?

Steve was perplexed and tried to cover for his outburst. "Sorry, Jack. You just startled me. A little jumpy after what happened. Yeah, it's terrible. Just terrible," Steve repeated, shaking his head. "Garrett of all people. Never did anything to anyone. It's a damn shame. I thought we lived in a safe neighborhood. Guess I should think again, huh?"

Chapter 18

Jack picked up Alex at 6:00 p.m. sharp without even going into the house to see the children. They were in good hands with Alex's mom, and seeing them would only make him want to stay.

They arrived at Alex's favorite restaurant, Joelle's, and as they walked in, three men spotted them and walked over. Alex had never seen them before and looked toward Jack to see if he knew them.

As they approached, the three men extended their arms toward Jack and all took part in a big bear hug. Alex's eyes shifted from her husband to the men, trying to figure out who they were. After about thirty seconds, Jack looked at Alex with a playful smirk and said, "Alex, I'd like you to meet my best friends, Sean, Dave, and Matt. Guys, this is my beautiful wife, Alex. She's been dying to meet you."

Alex cried tears of happiness after hugging the men. Her husband had kept this night a surprise for her. "When did you plan this?" she asked.

Dave answered for Jack. "We all met for a powwow last week during lunch hour and hammered out all of our differences. We were selfish jerks; we should've made time for your wedding. Now that you've met us…you may wish you never did!" he joked. "Jack's our best friend. We love him. Thanks for taking such good care of him while we were being self-centered. And by the way, I believe *congratulations* are in order! We can't wait to meet the twins!"

Alex was elated. All of her husband's outlandish behavior had been out of hurt from his friends, not toward her. That huge fight they had months ago when Jack had stormed off was legitimately because he was upset with his friends, and she had nagged him beyond belief.

She felt just awful for badgering him while he must have been dealing with the turmoil of potentially losing his lifelong buds. She made a mental note to apologize later that night.

They all sat down and enjoyed a hearty meal, along with some delicious red wine, laughter, and incredible conversation. It was like she'd known them her whole life, and she could tell Jack was thrilled to have his buddies back.

Other than Alex, each had quite a buzz on by the time they left, but the evening was superb. She couldn't wait to include Jack's friends in family parties and have them over, as she enjoyed catering to her guests. Life couldn't get any better than this.

As they proceeded to leave the restaurant, Alex hugged Jack's friends and promised to have them over within the next week. She sensed that Jack was in a great mood and pretended to be mad that he'd kept this a secret, though he knew she was ecstatic.

Once home, they were thrilled to see their little darlings safe and sound and fast asleep. After thanking Alex's mom for taking care of them, they decided to sit on the porch for a nightcap.

Jack told Alex of all the events of the day, explaining in detail all about Garrett's death and Jim's line of questioning. He started to tell her about the bullets in Steve's office but decided against it. It was probably nothing. Maybe he got a new hunting rifle and was excited and just had the bullets at work. He didn't want to make Alex nervous. Steve didn't have a bad bone in his body.

"What is it?" Alex asked him.

"What? What do you mean?"

"What is it?" she repeated. "You began to say something and then retracted it. Now you're fumbling with your jacket. What else were you going to say?"

"It's silly. Probably nothing." After a slight pause, he continued. He knew his wife well enough to know two things. One, she could read him like a book, and two, she would badger him until he admitted what he was about to say. She'd hound him until sunrise.

"Well, after Jim questioned us, I was in shock and a little, well, happy, as you know. I walked into Steve's office. Well, I should say, I barged in right after Jim left. As I did, I noticed Steve quickly hiding what I could swear were bullets in his desk.

"I didn't mean to walk in on him. I just wasn't thinking straight, but Steve kind of freaked out on me, which is highly unlike him. He apologized shortly thereafter, but it was strange."

He noticed his wife's face turn pale and added to his story. "Oh, you know what? It's nothing. A lot of people have guns. Some use them for hunting, others for protection. No big deal. I shouldn't have said anything."

"Yeah, you're right. It was probably nothing," Alex said, thinking back to that day in the office when she introduced Steve to her children. She got the chills all over again. "Jack, just...watch that guy, you know? I got a really weird feeling upon our last encounter, and I couldn't put my finger on it. I didn't say anything at the time-I thought maybe I was just tired, but something just might be a little off about him. Promise me you'll be careful, OK?"

"Don't worry about it. Let's just enjoy our wine, OK? Don't get all paranoid. Steve's a good guy. I've been working with him for years and have yet to see him get into an argument with anyone. Other than his small outburst with me, there's never been a reason not to trust the guy.

Today, he was probably just having a bad day, and he did apologize immediately. Finish up, and then let's go to bed. It's been a long day, and I'm exhausted."

Chapter 19

Nearly a week after Garrett's murder, Jack and Steve were still being instructed to stay in town. They were not quite suspects but were "persons of interest."

Jim became frustrated with all the formalities of building a case, but he honestly didn't think Jack had anything to do with it. Other than his missing watch from the John Doe crime scene, Jack really didn't fit the mold of the suspect. He openly admitted he hated Garrett but didn't show any violent streaks; just a man hating another man. Not everyone can get along.

Jim did have homicide detectives bring Steve in for formal questioning, however. Something was just not sitting right. Although Steve didn't appear to have any violent tendencies, he showed signs of intense anxiety during questioning—more than just the typical nervous reactions that innocent people display when under the gun.

As Jim asked more questions, Steve began to sweat and fidget a lot, and his story became jumbled every now and then regarding where he was the morning of the murder. He said he was with his cousin that morning but hesitated before giving his alibi, as if he had to think about it first.

Most of the police force that had interviewed him felt the same vibe when questioning Steve; however, they had no concrete evidence yet on which to build a case. Steve's alibi did check out, and there was no sign of the weapon. If he did commit the crime, he had shown great skill in hiding it. They would find something sooner or later, hopefully sooner.

Jim had a sick feeling that this person he used to work with could actually be their guy for both murders. Garrett had the same signature card on his person—that gruesome smile etched into his throat couldn't be mistaken. Whoever killed Garrett was the same person who had killed John Doe. When the pictures of both deceased men were compared side by side, it was a no-brainer. This was the same killer.

After interrogating Steve, Jim had an appointment to pay a visit to Garrett's sister, Priscilla. He wanted to ask her some questions about Garrett's life, and perhaps flash a picture of John Doe to see if Priscilla knew anything about him.

While happy that these cases were coming closer to fruition, sadly enough, Jim feared he might have to arrest his former co-worker if sufficient evidence pointed against him.

Chapter 20

Jim invited Priscilla to meet him for coffee and some breakfast in town. She was more than happy to oblige and jumped at the chance. She just wanted her brother's killer to be found so that she could give him a proper memorial and let him rest in peace. At the moment, that was her *only* goal.

They met at 8:00 a.m. at a little café on the other side of town. Jim extended his condolences and allowed some time for Priscilla to speak. She needed a strong shoulder to cry on and someone to listen to all of her concerns and grievances.

Once she had pulled herself together, Jim was able to delve into the personal life of Garrett. Then he explained that Garrett's killer had most likely killed John Doe as well.

"I have a photo of a man I'd like you to see and possibly identify if you recognize him," Jim said. "I must warn you, however, that it's a picture of him after he was murdered. Might be a little graphic for you. We never got identification on him; however, we think the murders might be linked. It's quite explicit, as there's a gunshot wound through his chest, but I'll try to cover that up for you. Would that be OK?"

"Sure. Whatever I can do to help."

He flipped the picture out of a manila folder and handed it to Priscilla. "Here it is. Do you happen to know this person?"

She took the picture in her hands and looked closely at the deceased man. Her eyes squinted a bit and then, almost instantly, widened with recognition.

"Oh, dear. I know him," Priscilla said, taking a sip of coffee. She nearly choked as she gulped it down. As tears built up in her eyes, she let out a sigh. "I guess for me to tell you who this is, I need to tell you a little more about Garrett. See, Garrett is—I mean, was—a homosexual. The person in this picture is his ex-boyfriend."

She paused a moment and then continued. "I didn't recognize him at first glance as it has been years since I've seen him. And, of course, he was alive. He was a lot thinner then, and I guess he had a bit more hair. They dated years ago, and I haven't seen or thought of him since. His name was Walter. The last name escapes me, but please give me a minute. I'm sure it'll come to me."

Her eyes started to swell up, and she looked like she was going to fall apart at any moment now. This was just too much for her to handle. She threw her head back and stared at the ceiling for a moment, swept away in some sort of short trance.

It was almost like swinging her head backward would cause the tears to fall back into their ducts and prevent them from falling again. When she lowered her head, she wiped her eyes, focused on Jim, and gave him the information he needed.

"Walter Reynolds." They dated maybe six or seven years ago, maybe longer. From what I remember, he was a nice person. Of course, he was about twenty or twenty-one when I met him. They got along really well but were still both hesitant about coming out of the closet.

Jim listened intently as she went on.

"We all knew, but their friends and most of Walter's family did not. They weren't going to accept this fact, and it was very stressful on their relationship."

"So what happened?"

"They decided to break it off and I know Garrett was devastated, even depressed at one point, but they both agreed it was the best thing for them. They did talk every now and again, just to check up on each other to see how they were doing. They really did care for each other a great deal."

Jim handed her a tissue. "I see. Thank you, Priscilla. I can't tell you how much that helps. Were he and his family close? Would they notice he was missing? No one came to claim his body. No one even inquired about him. People came to view his body, but it was never a match."

"He has family, but they live in the state of Washington. He moved here to go to college, and then when things didn't work out, he left to go back home. I'm sure the authorities in Washington were looking for him."

"Priscilla, was Garrett presently dating anyone?"

"Yes," she said, nodding. "As a matter of fact, he was. They were pretty serious, from what I understand. He's a bit older, but he works with him. His name is Steve Johnson, I believe."

Jim pondered this for a moment in disbelief. He had no idea. He was finally getting a bit of a break in the case. Steve had been appearing guiltier by the minute, and this last bit of information just sealed the deal. Jim was now convinced, without a shadow of a doubt, that his old co-worker was responsible for the murder of those two unfortunate men.

Just as the bill arrived, Jim's cell phone rang, displaying the phone number for police headquarters. "I'm sorry. I have to take this," he said to Priscilla. It was the chief, and he was frantic. "Jim, we need to find Steve and bring him in now. He's our man!"

He proceeded to tell Jim how Steve's cousin Randy, whom had acted as an alibi, showed up first thing that morning and admitted that he really wasn't with Steve the day of the murder. He thought Steve was innocent, so he went along with it. But now Steve was behaving strangely, and he just wasn't so sure. He had to confess the truth just in case, as the guilt was killing him.

Jim bowed his head, taking this all in. He was going to have to arrest Steve after all.

Chapter 21

"Alex, how about we go to a movie tonight?" Jack suggested. "We can get a babysitter. Maybe even go to dinner?"

"Should we?" she asked. "I mean, I hate leaving the twins. I think I'm addicted to them."

Jack just laughed at this. "They're fine! They're a year old now—practically able to take care of themselves," he joked.

Alex was feeding Amber peas and carrots, yet she was the one who almost wound up wearing it! Amber wasn't the neatest eater, and she managed to get food all over Alex and herself, not to mention the walls, the floor, and anything else that came across her path.

"Well, ok," Alex said, wiping Amber's mouth. "Sounds like a good idea. Let me just wash up and change my clothes. Can you call my parents and see if they can come over?"

"Sure. I'll tell them to come over at five."

Alex was excited. They didn't get to go on dates as often as they used to, but they felt like teenagers whenever they did. The last time they went out was the night of Garrett's murder—the same night Alex met Jack's wonderful friends.

She put on a beautiful black dress and got ready in minutes. As always, Jack was taken aback by her beauty when she entered the room. He was proud to show her off for their big night on the town.

They went to dinner at a popular Thai restaurant. She got the garlic spare ribs, and Jack ordered Thai chicken. They ate to their hearts' content, had some cocktails, and set out to go to the movie. They had an excellent time and swore to have a date night more often.

When they arrived home, they thanked Alex's parents and sat on the porch, as they usually did, while indulging in a nightcap of some delicious red wine. It was the perfect ending to a perfect evening. Little Kevin began crying, so Alex went inside to get him and have him sit outside with them. Amber was fast asleep.

The wind picked up and blew leaves and debris around in a small circle as the tree branches squeaked in a soft, eerie tone. Above them, they could barely see the clouds moving over a darkly lit sky.

"Looks like a storm might be moving in," said Jack. "Ready to go inside?"

"Sure, sounds good to me," said Alex, standing and collecting their glasses. "I'm tired anyway."

It was 10:00 p.m., and they were just about ready to call it a night when someone walked up to their driveway.

"Jack? Jack, is that you?" asked a male voice.

"Yep, it's me," Jack said, standing. "Who's there?" As he got a closer look, he thought it looked like his co-worker. "Steve? You OK? I didn't know you lived around here. Everything alright?"

"Sure. Everything's fine. Just walking around the neighborhood, getting some fresh air. It's a beautiful night. Hi, Alex. Is that Kevin with you?"

"Hi, Steve. Yes," Alex said. Waves of panic swept through her body as she embraced Kevin closer to her.

"I went for a long walk tonight. They say exercise is good for you. Supposed to keep you healthy and strong. I guess it's a way to guarantee a long life. At least that's what Garrett must've been thinking when he went for his morning jog. Didn't work out in his favor though, did it?"

He paused a moment, continuing when no one replied. "You never can tell which obstacles life is going to throw your way, can you? Fate decides how it will all wind up in the end. You can't change that."

Jack was obviously alarmed now.

"You're both really blessed. I wanted to adopt, you know, but never got to do it. As you know, Garrett and I were living together, at least on a part-time basis. We never got the chance. These adoption agencies don't make it easy for homosexual men to adopt. We would've made good parents. I'm sure of that."

"Um, Steve, I had no idea about you and Garrett, but it's getting late, and we just want to get some sleep," Jack said. "It was good seeing you, but I'll talk to you tomorrow at the office. You can tell me all about it then. It's not a good time right now. We need to get Kevin to bed. Good night Steve."

Steve resumed talking again as if Jack had never said a word. He moved back and forth, switching nervously from one foot to the other. "He was good to me, you know. But, he just kept asking about Walter and why he hadn't heard from him.

"Walter belonged in the past, where he should've stayed. He had to come looking for Garrett, though. Couldn't stay away. Pissed me off beyond belief. I tried to control my temper and figured he'd go back home eventually, but he stayed here for an entire week. I even spoke to him and gave him fair warning. He overstayed his welcome in this town as far as I'm concerned."

Alex began to tremble. They had no clue who Walter was, yet Steve referred to him as if they should know him. She would like to have said that Steve was just drunk, but he wasn't slurring his words. He was in complete control of his movements, aside from looking a bit nervous. She held Kevin tight to her body and grabbed Jack's arm.

"Steve, I'll see you tomorrow," Jack said, touching Alex's neck to gently push her inside.

"You saw the bullets, right Jack? I'm sure you must've told Alex about them too. They've been questioning me. I'm sure they've been questioning you, haven't they?" This was more of a statement than a question.

"I work really hard. I go to work every day. I don't think I've called in sick once during the past two or three years. I loved Garrett. I hated Walter. I'll admit to that wholeheartedly. He disrupted my life and caused a downward spiral.

"And by the way, I heard what you said about Garrett, even though I pretended to be on the phone. He wasn't useless, you know. He told me about the argument you guys had. I chose to stay out of it at the time. I figured you would both make up sooner or later. Guess not, huh?

"I'm also sorry I took your watch. I wore it once or twice, but then I lost it and just didn't have time to retrieve it. Sorry about that. Anyway, I'm not going down. I'm not going to jail. My life was taken just as Garrett's was. I'll never be able to adopt now. But the thing is, I am pretty sure I'm not going to jail."

"Steve, no one's going to jail," Jack said. "Yes, I told the police everything *I* know, which doesn't amount to much, but you're safe. They know you aren't guilty," he lied. He didn't realize he was lying until that precise moment. It was then that he realized Steve might very well be capable of killing Gar.

Jack turned and with one arm around his wife's waist and one hand on the door handle, he was almost safely inside the house when Steve pulled his hands out of his pockets.

Jack never saw it coming. Alex did. She screamed as Steve pulled the trigger on Jack first, leaving him to lie helplessly on the ground with a bullet in the back of his head and blood pooling all around him. He then meant to shoot Alex in the head as well, but she turned, causing him to hit her arm. He shot her again, rendering her unconscious.

Steve saw lights coming on in neighboring houses and knew he needed to get out of there in a hurry, but not before snatching Kevin from underneath Alex's body. Kevin was unscathed.

Chapter 22

The blaring sirens and bright flashing lights of police cars and other emergency vehicles arrived on the scene within ten minutes. Neighbors had heard the unmistakable sounds of gunshots and immediately called 911.

All of them appeared on their doorsteps, some afraid to come out for fear that the shooter may still be around. Others needed to find out what had happened regardless of the risk.

One neighbor was able to get a license plate of a car that had been parked only a block away. He was quite certain the suspect had fled in that direction right after the shooting.

As the police and ambulances arrived, the EMTs tried all available life-saving procedures to resuscitate Jack but were unable to do so. His life had been taken from him the moment the bullet entered his body. They pronounced him dead at 10:30 p.m.

Alex was still breathing, but her pulse was slight and she was unconscious. They rushed her to the nearest hospital and were able to stabilize her, though she was still deemed critically injured.

She had lost a lot of blood, but they were confident she would be OK physically. Once her pulse and blood pressure returned to safe levels, she should be in the clear. Mentally, however, she was going to need a lot of help.

They checked the house for anyone else and only found Amber, crying in her crib. They went to her immediately to make sure she wasn't hurt. She didn't appear to be, but they took her to the hospital anyway. They didn't know if the suspect had gone in the house at all and didn't want to take any chances.

Kevin was nowhere to be found.

The rescue teams lowered their heads as they feared their crime scene was about to go from bad to worse. Not only was the father dead, but the mother was in critical condition—and now the son appeared to have been kidnapped. Thankfully, their daughter was unharmed, but their lives would never be the same.

Investigators left on the scene performed a thorough search for any evidence left behind, anything that would lead them to the shooter.

They found a phonebook inside the house and scanned it for any friends or relatives of Alex and Jack. Alex's parents' phone number was listed, and an officer called immediately to notify them of Alex's condition and tell them which hospital she was in.

He didn't tell them about their dead son-in-law or their missing grandchild over the phone, responding to their questions only by telling them that someone would meet them at the hospital with more information.

They interviewed neighbors one by one. No one really saw anything, but each one accurately described the loud, piercing blasts that couldn't be mistaken for anything other than gunshots.

Even though it was late, no one on the block was going to be able to sleep. The lights on the emergency vehicles lit up the entire area like a Christmas tree, and everyone was in shock at the events that had transpired.

Some were closer to Jack and Alex than others, but everyone agreed they were likable, respectable people. Kevin and Amber were adorable, and since they were the only toddlers on the block, they got tons of attention.

It was hard to believe this could have happened. Some were fearful that it was a random shooting and that it could have happened to any one of them. They wondered what had caused the shooter to single out Alex and Jack. Was it just because they were the only ones outside? Or was it a targeted shooting?

The officers on the scene promised to get them more details as soon as they uncovered them and implored everyone to go back inside and catch some sleep.

The squad cars would be circling the area all night, so their safety was guaranteed.

After a few hours, the last of the neighbors went inside, praying for the Rider family and hoping that at least Alex would survive and Kevin would be found, alive and unharmed, very soon.

Chapter 23

The license plate came back registered to Steve Johnson, but Steve Johnson was long gone. Investigators issued an alert for all cars matching that description that included instructions to pay special attention to a one-year-old boy in the passenger seat.

After two days in the hospital, Alex started to wake up. The nurses were in her room at the time, as was her mother, father, and brother. Her mother was holding Amber in her lap.

"What happened?" she whispered.

"How do you feel, sweetheart?" her mom asked, trying to stall as much as possible.

"Mom? Where's Jack?" She looked at Amber in her mother's arms. "Where's Kevin?" Her voice was in a pronounced panic now. Desperately pleading. She tried to ease herself up on the pillow but couldn't find the strength to do so. She turned toward the unoccupied bed in the room, questions flooding her mind.

"Alex, please take it easy," her mother said. "You've been through a lot. You need to recuperate. First things first." Her mother stood next to her bed now, fiddling with the edge of the sheets as if somehow, that would make the pain go away.

She poured a small glass of water for Alex from the tiny yellow pitcher on the table beside the bed. Although Alex didn't want any of it, her mother felt better just doing anything to try to help.

Her father came over to hold his daughter's hand. As she looked toward her brother, she noticed his eyes were bloodshot and he looked as though he hadn't slept in a week. He even looked sympathetic. Her brother had never been sympathetic for as long as he had been alive.

She then began to remember. Memories started pouring in; the irreparable flood gates had burst opened.

"Mom? Where are they?!" She was screaming now.

Her father cradled her head and her mother sat on the bed with her. Her brother turned his head as she watched him wipe away tears from his bloodshot eyes. The nurses left the room but motioned that they would be waiting just outside the door.

"Alex, there was an incident two nights ago. We don't know all the details. We hope you can shed some light if you remember; however, the police are working full-time trying to catch the guy."

"Steve," Alex said. "His name is Steve. He worked with Jack. Now, where is Jack?" Tears were flowing steadily now.

Her mom took a deep breath and looked Alex in the eyes. "Alex, honey, Jack was shot. When the paramedics arrived at your house, they tried everything. They really did. There was just nothing they could do. He was already…gone."

"Nooooooo! No! Not Jack. Not Jack, Mom. No!" She motioned for Amber. Her mother quickly handed her over and Alex hugged her daughter close. "Mom, where is Kevin? Oh my God. Where is *Kevin*?"

"Alex, the police have an alert out looking for him now," her mother said. "Apparently this Steve fellow kidnapped Kevin. We're going to find him, honey. I promise. We'll find him."

"He's *missing?!*" Alex was hysterical now. Amber started crying as well, rubbing her eyes with her two little fists. The nurses came in to give Alex a sedative, as she was still in a weakened condition and needed to rest in order to get well.

With all of her strength, she tried to fight off the sedative and pull herself up to a sitting position in an effort to go and single-handedly find her son, but the powerful narcotic was stronger and effortlessly won the battle. Within minutes, Alex was fast asleep.

Chapter 24

A state-wide manhunt was underway, consisting of every officer the department could spare. The car Steve had originally driven was found abandoned in an inconspicuous wooded area. Using their best efforts, investigators combed the car for any evidence or clues that might lead them to Steve's next destination.

They tried to find Steve's family members or friends and again came up blank. He had kept his private, violent life a dark secret from everyone he knew.

At a nearby store, a well-meaning clerk said she thought someone resembling Steve had come in for a few baby items and some food, but she couldn't be sure. She couldn't make a positive identification.

They checked all reports on recently stolen cars or license plates, but no positive matches turned up. They showed photographs at the train and bus stations, but so much traffic goes through those that it would take a miracle for someone to recall seeing them. Even if they did, they would also need to remember their destination to be of much use, and there was no chance in hell of that happening.

Jim was beside himself. If only he had sped up the initial investigation on Steve by one day, he could have been locked up. Jack would be alive, and Kevin would be safe and sound in his mother's arms. Chances are that Jack never would've known Steve had intended on targeting him.

If Jim had been able to track down Steve after his conversation with Garrett's sister that very same day, none of this would've happened. He didn't even think to warn Jack or that he would be in any kind of imminent danger. In Jim's eyes, both Walter and Garrett's murders were due to some sort of obsessive love triangle—a crime of passion. There was no apparent reason that Jack would've been involved.

Jim spent one too many evenings drowning his sorrows in a bottle of scotch before realizing he needed to give it his all if they were to find this creep. There was no use wallowing in "what-ifs" right now. There would be plenty of time for self-pity once this psychopath was found. There was nothing he could do now about the past. The only thing he could do was try to move forward in order to fix the future.

How does a man that has worked at the same company for years without a trace of violence turn out to be a serial killer? How did no one have a clue about his relationship with Garrett? How do you go from having a decent life to becoming a hunted fugitive? Jim knew the answer to the questions, although he didn't want to believe it. Steve had never been a decent man. He'd had everyone fooled, including Jim.

This shouldn't have surprised him, however, as sociopaths are known to behave like normal, even likable, people. It's when you really get to know them on an intimate level that the truth starts spilling out like a leaky faucet. Steve kept to himself at work, making it easy to just blend in with the crowd.

All Symmetry employees who were questioned about Steve said the same thing: He was a nice, quiet man in the accounting department. He came in on time and left on time. He always brought a bagged lunch, socialized with no one, and didn't cause any trouble. No one even knew that he and Garrett were gay, much less an item.

He wasn't only book smart, but apparently, he also knew how to manipulate. That combination was the essential building blocks for a disaster.

Now to find out he's most likely killed twice, that they knew of, and had recently made his third kill? Add to his repertoire a kidnapping, and he would be facing back-to-back life sentences. That is, if they found him.

They had to find him. A child's life was at stake. He couldn't hurt a child, could he?

Chapter 25

Alex woke up after the combination of pain killers and sedatives had worn off. Only her mom and Amber were in the room with her. Her father and brother had gone home to get some rest. Jack's parents had come by to see her, but she was sleeping when they arrived. They left some flowers and shared some grieving time with Alex's mom. They promised to come by later that week.

Amber was still too young to understand what was going on or the importance and devastation that this would have upon her young life.

Physically, Alex was in much better shape today compared to yesterday and appeared just a little bit stronger. She had some color in her cheeks and was a bit more focused.

As she woke up, she kept her eyes closed for a brief moment in an effort to get her thoughts together, recalling the words she had once read from an anonymous quote: "Sometimes, you can see the world clearer with your eyes closed." As she opened them, she saw her mom facing the hospital room window, balancing a cup of coffee in one hand and a bagel in the other.

"Mom? I need a favor."

"Oh, honey, I didn't realize you were up," her mother said, spinning around, eager to help in any way. "Sure, what do you need?"

"I need to go find Kevin. Today. I need to get up out of bed, get dressed, and find him. He's your grandson too. Don't you *want* to find him? Why is everyone just sitting around *me?*" Her voice climbed from composed to borderline hysterical.

"Alex, sweetheart, the police are working overtime to find him. We have to put our trust in them. There's nothing that you or I or anyone can do. All we can do now is pray. It's out of our hands."

Alex was too weak to put up a fight. As frantic as she was, she didn't possess the strength or the energy to find her little boy. With each passing day, she felt as if she was dying inside, not knowing where he was. She longed to feel his little hands and have his eyes stare up at her with complete and total trust. She had let him down.

Amber had started asking for her father and Kevin, breaking Alex's heart even more. She couldn't bear the thought of losing her son and husband, but this was the first time she had thought about how this would affect Amber.

Alex was sinking into a deep depression, and the doctors and family were all concerned. She had no interest in eating, and the only thing that kept her going was her beautiful, innocent daughter—who was destined to mourn her father and twin brother the rest of her life.

After about a one-week hospital stay, doctors signed the release forms allowing Alex to go home, under the stipulation that she would have someone with her each day and night to help her for at least another week.

This put her in somewhat of a better mood until it dawned on her that she would be going to a place where her husband was murdered and her child, as well as her life as she knew it, was stolen right from under her. The place that held so many good memories would now seem foreign and tragic.

She daydreamed back to less than two years ago when she had shared the news of her pregnancy with Jack. She recalled when they had signed the papers to buy the house, how happy they were. Finally, she thought of the bar in which they'd met, the conversation that had kept her out past curfew, and the everlasting kiss that had made her fall in love with Jack.

All of this was too much to bear. Once she got into her parents' car, she buried her face in Amber's hair and sobbed uncontrollably. She had finally succumbed to the grief that had been accumulating daily in the hospital.

As they pulled up to the driveway, she felt her heart break once again. She looked at the porch where her husband took his final breath. Now that she was home, his funeral would have to be planned. His parents took the liberty of doing this for her. She simply wasn't up to it.

The funeral took place two days later, on Thursday. Alex and Amber sat in the back seat of the limousine with Jack's parents. There were still no leads on Kevin's whereabouts, and Alex was falling apart at the seams. She prayed for what seemed like every minute of every day that they would find her son alive and unharmed.

At the funeral home, Alex and Amber looked at Jack one last time. Alex touched his hand and kissed his lips and eyes. She looked at the wedding ring on his finger and traced the outline of it with her own. She watched as Amber touched her daddy's hand and felt Amber bury her face in her shoulder.

Alex's father came over and helped her get up from the kneeler. They stood there in silence, saying a prayer over her deceased husband. Alex remained calm only due to the sedatives that had been prescribed to her. It would only be a matter of time before she cracked.

After the wake, they arrived at the cemetery, where Alex watched as her husband's coffin was lowered into the ground. She said a few short prayers and promised him she'd find Kevin—a promise she knew in her heart she couldn't keep.

Chapter 26

A year passed, and the authorities advised Alex that the chances of finding Kevin's body were slim to none. The chances of finding him alive were even smaller. Though she already knew this, having someone confirm it drove a stake through her severely broken heart. She had given a memorial in honor of her missing son but still had kept a glimmer of hope that he would be found—possibly even found alive.

She had been in counseling since the day she regained her strength. She tried her best to accommodate Amber and make her life as normal as possible. Amber had cried for her father for the first few months, but that eventually dwindled away. Kevin was another story. Amber had asked for him up until two months ago, when Alex removed his pictures from her sight just to give Amber a chance to heal.

Her life wasn't starting off in the best of circumstances. Not only had she lost her father and twin brother, but her paternal grandparents had also recently passed away.

Jack's father and mother were on their way back from the supermarket when Jack's father suffered a massive heart attack while driving.

He had been complaining of severe chest pains a few days prior but later claimed that they had subsided. The autopsy showed that he'd died instantly from heart failure, losing control of the car and causing it to cross three lanes, crashing into a cement divider on the busy highway. In the midst of the crash, an oncoming car hit the passenger side door at seventy-five miles per hour. Jack's mother was killed upon impact.

From that point on, Alex made a conscious decision that she had to do whatever was necessary to enable Amber to lead a happy, somewhat normal life. She had a hard time convincing her family to go along with her plan, but they would have to respect her wishes. She simply wouldn't have it any other way.

She asked her mom to babysit Amber while she went through the deserted house and removed any traces of Kevin. She went through his dresser drawers and brought his clothes up to her nose to try to smell any last scent of her baby boy.

After about three hours of cleaning up his things, she collapsed on the floor of his room holding his favorite blanket and sobbed in long, drawn-out screams.

She knew what she was doing was morally incorrect, but she had to go through with it. She had chosen to hide the fact that Kevin ever existed from Amber—a decision that had crushed Alex but that, in her mind, was the only thing that would help Amber in the long run.

In order for this to work, she needed to involve her parents and brother with this deception as well. It wouldn't be easy, but she didn't want to put Amber through any more pain.

At first they didn't agree with her, even fighting her tooth and nail, but after some persistent persuasion, they gave in. They wanted their daughter and granddaughter's life to be as painless as possible, and if this was going to help, then they felt they had no choice but to oblige. Alex's parents kept Kevin's memory alive with photographs in their bedroom, a place where Amber was never permitted to go.

After going through all of his things, Alex felt a piece of herself die along with her missing son.

PART II

*Dreams are the mind's protective interpretation
of the harsh reality that is most often feared.*

Chapter 27

THIRTEEN YEARS LATER

It was Thursday night, and Amber had gone to her best friend Tiffany's house as she had always done for the past five years. It was the one night they got to lounge on the couch, eat potato chips with homemade dip, watch television, and just talk about the seemingly normal, important things that fifteen-year-olds do.

Except Amber wasn't a normal fifteen-year-old. That idea got blown away about the same time her father had, fourteen years earlier. Her memories of her father were obsolete. She sometimes conjured up false memories of the man she wished to be her father, but she could never truly remember. Though she knew it was impossible, she sometimes felt his presence or thought that a particular aftershave cream smelled pleasantly familiar; therefore, it must have been his.

She had one piece of his clothing that her mother kept; it was his favorite shirt—a light blue, button-down, short-sleeved shirt with a pocket on the left-hand side. It wasn't anything fancy; quite the opposite, but Amber's mother said he wore it all the time. It had since been washed, but Amber dreamt she could still smell his clean scent.

There were times she wished she could speak to him and ask him the questions she never got to ask. What was his favorite color? What flavor ice cream did he like? Did he even *like* ice cream? What was his favorite movie, band, or song? Was she the apple of his eye for the one short year that he knew her? Did he sing her to sleep or tell bedtime stories? There were times when Amber just sat alone at night and watched her parents' wedding video over and over again, if only to take comfort in her father's voice and unique mannerisms.

She knew nothing about the man she dreamt about at night. She had no clue why, but she loved him so much it hurt. She'd always had this feeling of a nagging void.

People lose their parents all of the time, and they get over it, but she just felt that at times, she was losing her grip. She'd smile and put up a believable façade, but sometimes it was all she could do to keep from having a meltdown.

She shook her head and interrupted her own thoughts. If she focused on them too long, she'd get lost in a downward spiral of self-pity and deep depression. The only way to overcome this feeling of dread was to change the subject. "What do ya feel like watching tonight? Want to put a movie in, Tiff?"

"Sure. We need some chips and dip. Want a Pepsi?"

Amber nodded and smiled.

As Tiffany returned with all of their goodies, Amber first hesitated and then asked a random question that had been nagging her for quite some time. "Hey, kind of a weird question, but, do you dream much? I mean, do you remember your dreams?"

"Sure. Doesn't everyone dream? I mean, nothing that's worth repeating the next day, but yea, I have dreams here and there. Just the normal stuff. You know, like it was me but it wasn't me type stuff." She laughed. "I think last night I dreamt that my dog was doing my book report. How's that for wishful thinking? How about you?"

"Yes!" said Amber. "So much that it's becoming kind of freaky. Almost too real. I've woken up at times running through the halls or screaming, or both. It's getting worse as the years go on."

"Really? Well, that's not necessarily *the most horrible* thing in the world, but I could see how that is disturbing. OK, so, what did you dream of last night?" Tiffany was a good listener, even as she crunched away on potato chips.

"Hmm...last night. I dreamt I was walking down the street when a bunch of monkeys, about ten of them, swarmed in front of me. They jumped into my arms."

"Monkeys, huh? Hmm. So, you're afraid of monkeys?"

"No. No, it was actually cute," Amber said.

"OK, sooo?"

"So then as quickly as they jumped in my arms, they jumped out and ran to the house on the side of the road. When I looked, there were adult monkeys stepping out of a minivan, dressed in suits and dresses. The baby monkeys jumped into their arms."

"So, you were jealous. Is that it?" She joked.

"Yeah, I was jealous," she answered sarcastically. "Forget it, you're missing the point."

"Okay, seriously, what point are you trying to make? You had a dream about monkeys. Unless you're afraid of monkeys, I don't see how this dream was scary. I'm sorry; maybe I'm missing something." Tiffany started to laugh but realized it might not be the most appropriate moment.

Amber looked as though she were about to cry. She got up from her chair, grabbed a handful of chips, and overloaded them with dip. After she stuffed them into her mouth and chewed for a minute, she said, "That dream didn't bother me. It's the other ones that do. You asked me what I dreamt of last night. Last night, all I dreamt about was monkeys."

"OK, I'm sorry. I'm a slow learner. Let's start over. Can you give me an example of a non-primate-related dream?" She was trying to getting her friend to laugh, but it was going to be a little tougher than usual this evening.

Amber shot her a look of slight annoyance and answered, "Well, ugh. I guess so. The other night, I had a dream that I was climbing a ladder. I was in some sort of warehouse, and I was climbing a ladder to nowhere, really. You know how I'm afraid of heights."

Tiffany nodded, encouraging Amber to continue.

"The warehouse was really dark, but I was still able to see. The walls were a dull grey, very depressing. When I reached the top of the ladder, I stepped off and was in the middle of some party. It was still the warehouse; just now everything was a bit more perky and white, instead of the dreary grey.

"There were tables with white tablecloths and people all sitting around talking and laughing. And then, there was my dad, right in front of me. I tried to talk to him, but he acted as if he saw me every day and that it wasn't really all that important to talk to me. I only wanted a few minutes, ya know?

"Anyway, I approached some of the tables and felt compelled to touch the shirt sleeve of the person sitting there. She just laughed this hearty, unforgettable laugh. Not quite evil, but it was somewhat condescending. She then looked at the person next to her and said, "She thinks we're ghosts."

"Sorry to interrupt, but that's weird stuff, girl," Tiffany said, wide eyed. "But go on. I like it."

"Tell me about it. So, there's a kid up there too. He's about my age. Looks like me too. I feel like I should know him, kind of like I recognize him but don't know who he is. I see my dad again, and I'm trying to talk to him, but still, he's too busy.

"It went on like that for what seemed like minutes, and then my father finally came over to me. It was the end of the dream. He started talking and dictated a note to my mother somehow that said to tell you that your cousin, Tom, is in good hands."

Tiffany and her cousin Tom were extremely close. They were the same age and went to the same school. He constantly shielded her from the mean kids at school and always made sure she got home safely each and every day. If he didn't have a ride, he would walk with her to school. If he had a ride, he made sure to swing by and pick Tiffany up as well.

During the summer, a few of his friends had gotten their licenses and they went for a drive late at night. The driver was a good kid but fell asleep behind the wheel. All of the kids survived with minor injuries, except for Tom. He hung on for as long as he could but died three hours later in the hospital due to severe head injuries. There was nothing that could have been done to save his life. The doctors tried everything.

Amber looked at Tiffany, and now she was the one almost in tears. "I'm so sorry," Amber said. "I didn't mean to upset you but, I had to share it with you. It was all so spooky—calming and weird at the same time. I know it's just a dream, but ya see what I'm saying? They're so vivid, so real. They're not just bizarre…They almost make sense."

"It's OK," Tiffany said, wiping her eyes. "I'm not upset with you. I was really intrigued. Ya know, like I was watching a movie. I wanted to hear all of it. I just wasn't prepared for that type of ending. Weird, but yea, comforting. It's OK, Amber. I'm not mad. It was just a dream."

"Yeah, I'm sorry to bother you with all of my bullshit," Amber said. "Let's put a movie in. Sound like a plan?"

"*Yes*! We have plenty of snacks." At this they both giggled and put in one of their all-time favorites, *"Desolation."* They loved scary movies.

"Hey, why don't you sleep over tonight?" Tiffany suggested. "I have clothes you can borrow for school tomorrow. Think your mom will allow it? I mean, it *is* a school night." They both rolled their eyes, acknowledging the rules.

"Sure. I just have to sound groggy when I call her and tell her we're going to sleep *now*. Otherwise, she'll never let me." They giggled some more as Amber called her mom and got permission to stay over.

Chapter 28

"Tiff, are you up?"

Tiffany opened her eyes to see Amber standing a foot away from her, staring down at her.

"Sheesh, Amber. I am now. What's wrong?" she asked, sitting up. "You scared the hell out of me. You sound wide awake."

"That's because I *am*. Sorry. OK, *this* one was really strange. It was *so* real. I feel like there's some type of meaning to it that I just can't explain. This is what you get for asking me to stay over."

It was 3:00 a.m., and all Tiffany *really* wanted to do was get some quality sleep. She had a killer exam tomorrow, and they'd gone to bed pretty late for a school night. Amber was her best friend, however, and she needed to talk. This was what best friends did. They talked.

"OK. You got my full attention. Let's hear it," Tiffany said, rubbing her eyes to try and fully wake up. She was trying to focus the best she could.

"OK, here goes." Amber revealed the dream as if she were a narrator telling a ghost story at a campfire site.

"For many years, my mom has kept this beautiful figurine near the kitchen telephone. It's as odd as it is beautiful. To describe it is somewhat difficult, but I'll certainly give it a try. The figurine is about the size of my hand."

She opened up her palm as she described it.

"In the center is an Asian-type fabric made of pinkish silk embroidered with flowers in the center. It looks like a delicate bow. From the center, stretching outward on both sides, are four dark black silhouettes. They are velvety to the touch. In my dream, no one had ever really asked what the figurine is, nor has anyone ever cared."

"Interesting," said Tiffany, wide awake now. "Really. You've got my undivided attention."

"I should. You're in the dream with me. You're in my dreams a lot, come to think of it. Anyway, you and I were in the woods outside the house. As you know, there's not anything outside that's dangerous or poisonous, which is why I was so shocked upon first glance. It was moving toward us faster and faster.

"In the woods was a *huge*, black, hairy, creepy tarantula. It must've *easily* been the size of my hand, though, even in my dream, I didn't stick around to find out. It looked as though it had some private aspiration to capture us in one of its vicious webs.

"You know how I'm afraid of a tiny house spider. I ran like my life depended on it into the house to tell my mom what we'd seen in the yard. You were right behind me."

"Did I ever tell you that you're a bit spooky?" Tiffany interrupted. "Not that I don't like it, though."

"Gee, thanks, there's more though. So, my mom was at the neighbor's house, and our only two choices were the obvious: Wait to warn her, or just call her. I decided just to call her and tell her. As I reached for the telephone, I only then noticed that the peculiar figurine wasn't there...well, not entirely there.

"All that was left in its place was the stand that had held it. To my knowledge, it had never been empty before. As I stood studying it, I was distracted.

"I saw it crawling up the wall. Into the stand it went and stretched its legs outward on both sides—eight dark black silhouettes. The tarantula. It came back and enclosed its body within its own web; an intricate pink, delicate, beautiful bow handcrafted by none other than the creepy crawler itself. At that precise moment, my mom walked into the house."

"Wow," said Tiffany, taking it all in for a moment. "First monkeys, and now spiders? I have to say, it's definitely a weird dream, but it's also almost—forgive me for sounding a bit corny—poetic. A tarantula has never, in my mind, been beautiful, but the way you described it in the figurine is almost calming."

"I know! Both dreams were so eerie, but almost, I don't know, soothing. It felt like the tarantula had relevance, like it was supposed to mean something to me."

"Hmm. Sounds like some dream therapy is called for. What do you think? I mean, the dream about your father is pretty self-explanatory. I don't think you need to go to a shrink to figure out that you miss your father. But the spider dream. Hmm. What's that all about? Something like, "When you start spinning lies—sort of like a web of deceit? Or is it that you just want to have a pet spider?"

They burst out in laughter, and Amber's laughing turned into a loud snorting sound every few moments. They were extremely tired and too giddy for a serious conversation. Tiffany could always bring out the immature side of Amber. For just a few short moments, their lives were without worries and heartache. They chatted a little more and were able to doze off for the remainder of the night.

The next morning, Amber recalled her dream and couldn't shake its creepy memory.

Chapter 29

It was very dark, pitch black actually, but Zach had grown so accustomed to darkness that it had become more of a comfort to him than something to fear.

Many people would become paranoid, even come close to suffering heart failure, if they had to endure the eerie black walls that surrounded him almost every night. And if the darkness alone wasn't enough to frighten them, the high-pitched sounds would send chills running through their veins, at first only causing goose bumps.

But after a few minutes of trying to decipher which animal or insect was making each horrific sound, the ordinary person would feel the hair on their neck rising and become terrified with the realization of their own mortality.

While sight and sound are two senses heavily relied upon by most people, one can never take for granted the sense of touch. Zach learned this many years ago—eleven to be exact. The first time he felt a spider crawl up his arm, he was overcome with panic.

If it were just one, it might not have been so terrible. But it wasn't one. It was more than that. A lot more. There had to have been at least thirty. As he frantically tried to brush them off, it seemed that ten more appeared instantaneously. He may have been able to deal with it if he'd been awake, but instead he was in a dead sleep, only to be awoken by the light, feathery tickling of these eight-legged arachnids.

For as long as he could remember, he had lived inside the walls of some type of dark, desolate dwelling. Now, he found just as much solace in a cave as he did in a house. Zach's current home was in the downstairs portion of an old stucco building whose elderly landlords had only come to visit once in five years.

Appearing a lot older than he actually was, he'd fooled this couple for the past two years, telling them that he was fifteen years old when they'd met, when in reality, he was only thirteen at the time. He now alternated between this place he called home and the dark caves that stood only miles away.

For the most part, he only spent the nights in the caves when he disposed of his victims and found himself too tired to make his way "home." On those nights, he parked his old, beaten down vehicle and made the walk through the canyons carrying his victim, relying on the strength of his muscular shoulders for leverage.

His powerfully built physique was a contributing factor to his older appearance. He also wasn't awkward like most fifteen-year-olds and exuded pure confidence in anything he did.

As he carried his victim, he took note of the sights surrounding him. Here in the desert, the moon illuminated from overhead; a flashlight wasn't necessary to guide him on his walk, though he always brought one just in case.

There was no need for him to actually bury the bodies. In the distance, he'd hear the coyotes howling their evening tune, probably smelling the scent of their banquet about to arrive. He left his victims in a desolate area for the wildlife to devour.

He burned their clothes to mere shreds and threw any of their personal items down the drain pipes in the street, never to be seen again. He didn't keep any souvenirs, nor did he sell any of the victims' personal items. He killed for the simple sport of it. He would, however, take any money they had, just to pay for gas for his car and part of the rent.

His victims never committed any major crimes, and he was not a vigilante by any means, but the rest of the world had deprived him of a normal life, and someone had to pay.

He had learned to survive on little. His meals consisted of the very coyotes that fed upon his victims, and he wasn't averse to eating rabbits and lizards as well. He trapped all his "meals" by himself and was quite proud of his divine cooking skill in his make-shift kitchen that consisted of a decent-sized toaster oven, a two-burner stove, and a practical mini-fridge.

Money wasn't a worry, as he had never been fortunate enough to understand the materialistic luxuries of life. His only bills were rent, some gas money, and a little bit of food. He needed his car for hiding his victims during transport.

He has learned to do odd jobs that paid cash so that he never has to show proper identification. He did have to shave and make himself look presentable. When necessary, he acquired most of his decent-looking clothes by stealing them off some of his victims, just so he had something nice to wear in order to fool the rest of society.

During the day he slept in his humble abode, and at night he blended in perfectly with the darkness. He was always comforted by the black of night, never looking forward to seeing the light of day. He wasn't a vampire, neither were his skin or eyes sensitive to light; he simply found solace in blending with the shadows.

At one time, there had been a man providing him with food and shelter, but he had since left this world to venture into another. Zach helped send him there by pushing him down a flight of stairs five years ago in the run-down projects they called home.

They had never actually lived in a decent home, but this person, whom Zach called "Joe," found them shelter and food every once in a while. He was quite certain that "Joe" wasn't his real name, but he didn't care. The man answered to it.

By the time Zach was about ten, Joe had showed him all the essential things there were to know about life. He could only estimate his own age, as there were no records dating back to when he was born.

Joe had shared some survival techniques with him. He'd shown him how to read and write, how to take a beating, how he was supposed to put up with the sexual abuse Joe forced upon him, how to steal, how to lie, and, more importantly, he'd shown him how to kill. The last part was what had helped Zach survive the last five years.

Joe was Zach's first real kill. He couldn't really take all of the credit, however, as Joe was permanently drunk. He could barely balance himself on his own two feet and often depended on Zach to be his human crutch, and Zach hadn't actually *intended* to kill him.

One night Joe got a little too drunk, which was quite common, but he was way too abusive for even Zach to handle. Although his main objective wasn't to actually kill Joe, it worked out to his favor. He had only meant to push Joe off of him in self-defense.

They happened to be standing at the top of the stairs, and Zach gave a good push, followed by a swift kick in the knees. Years of abuse had come together to give him the adrenalin rush he needed to fight back. Joe lost his balance and reached out to Zach, who promptly backed away, offering no assistance.

Zach was frozen, partly in horror and partly curious about what would happen. Joe tried to reach for the railing and regain his balance, but he was just too intoxicated. By the time he had rolled all the way to the bottom of the stairwell, his body had twisted and contorted way too many times.

Zach heard the startling *"snap"* of his neck and never forgot that fateful, final sound. He descended the stairs in slow motion, hesitating on each step and tightly grabbing onto the rails on his way down.

When he finally reached the bottom, he whispered Joe's name, knowing for certain he wouldn't get a response. Joe's eyes were wide open, and his face was visibly disfigured. Although he was only ten, Zach knew very well what death was, and this was as close as he had ever gotten on his own.

After he overcame the initial shock of Joe's demise, he found that he kind of liked it. It made him feel powerful and in full control—a feeling he had never experienced before in his short life.

Though he'd grown quite accustomed to his life, he felt at one point like there was something more. Maybe not in this life, maybe in a past life, but definitely at one point.

He once read a book describing how certain things that you feel or think about, without reason or logical explanation, similar to déjà vu, may be due to the fact that they happened to you in a *past* life. He wasn't sure how much he actually believed that, but sometimes, it helped him to get by. If Zach ever needed a bit of comfort, that theory helped him achieve it.

He wondered if it were possible that he was ever loved by what the commoners called parents. If Joe was his father, he had to have had a mother at one point. Did Joe kill her? Did she die of natural causes? Was she still alive? Was she nice to him? He wanted to believe she was.

His only friend was what used to be his enemy—a nice, giant-sized tarantula. Since his first encounter with spiders in his younger years, Zach made it a point to respect all kinds of eight-legged creatures.

One day, he had confiscated a large fish tank from the end of someone's driveway, getting ready to be picked up by the garbage men. He didn't know why, but he felt he should have it, so he brought it with him to his home.

Within about two weeks, he felt the need to get himself a "pet." On one of his trips to his personal graveyard, he picked one up. It wasn't what most people call the conventional pet, but to Zach, it was beautiful.

He actually felt a little guilty removing this pet from his natural habitat, where he already had spun his webs and created his natural spider decor—but not guilty enough to leave him alone.

He transported the tarantula from the desert to his home in a tiny sauce jar he'd found on the street. They hit if off right away. The tarantula didn't even try to bite him. He then transferred him from the sauce jar to the fish tank and, watching him walk around, decided on a name. He liked the name Hank. "Hank is in the tank," he thought. This was enough to initiate a small chuckle—something that was few and far between.

Chapter 30

After Joe's unfortunate accident, Zach felt the incessant need to kill again. By age fifteen, due to the lifetime of abuse that had turned him into a heartless monster, he had killed over ten people—some male, some female.

Tonight, he felt that tension that always preceded one of his killing binges. Usually, his "kill of choice" consisted of any individual who might have given him a poor attitude or flashed him an undeserved dirty look. This individual never did anything that would constitute a reason to be killed, but in Zach's mind, he didn't require justification. He abided by his own rules and didn't need to answer to anyone.

Tonight's victim turned out to be an unsuspecting woman. Zach was heading out for an evening walk, as he always did once the sun went down. Here in the desert, the temperature could range from fifty to eighty degrees in a single day. The cool, brisk air of this particular evening was something Zach looked forward to during this time of year.

As he set foot on the pavement, he caught eyes with a beautiful woman who was around twenty-five or twenty-six years of age. He knew he didn't really come across like an attractive man, especially since he hadn't slept in a while and his clothes were not stylish in the least. He only had a few good outfits that could be considered fashionable and those needed to be saved for special occasions, such as the infrequent times that he worked.

Despite his undesirable upbringing, Zach was an especially good-looking teenager. When he did clean himself up and catch sight of himself in a mirror, he had to admit that he could pass for a normal, handsome teenage boy. At times, he found himself pretending he was.

He flashed a smile at the woman, not because he felt like being uncharacteristically friendly but because he was curious. He wanted to see how she would react to a teenager who appeared to be nice. Little did she know that her reaction would be the deciding factor on whether she lived a glorious, fulfilling life or died a horrific death.

As he smiled at her, she squinted her eyes as if he'd said something perverse or offensive. With that, she glared at him as though he had some nerve and began to meander off.

It was to his advantage that there were no real bystanders on the street that night. It was to her disadvantage that she had chosen to walk on this particular street. Sometimes the poor, meaningless choices that are made in life are the ones that matter most.

He ran to catch up to her and gently tapped her on the shoulder. She turned abruptly and grabbed onto her purse. "Can I help you?" she asked in the most stern, condescending tone she could muster.

Zach stared into her eyes briefly and relished in the moment. He was indecisive on how to handle this one. Should he say something cool and threatening, sort of like a one-liner from a James Bond movie? Or, should he not say anything at all and leave her wondering what her fate was?

He chose to say *something*. The temptation was just too great. "Ma'am? You cannot help me, but thank you for asking. It's a shame too, 'cause a minute ago, you did have the utmost opportunity to help yourself. You made the wrong decision, and now that moment is gone. Because of your scowling face and look of disgust, you gave me a very legitimate reason to do what I need to do."

He looked around to see if there was anyone close enough to be a witness to his next move. His home was only two blocks away, and he was used to carrying bodies much farther. Nobody was around. This was just too perfect.

She stared at him, horrified now—and rightfully so. She turned to take a step away and planned on running, assuming that she was faster than he was, but Zach didn't give her a moment's chance. With a swift chop to the neck, he knocked the wind out of her, forcing her to pass out on the spot.

He lifted her limp body up and draped her over his shoulder. As he passed people farther down the street, he mumbled to himself, but loudly enough for others to hear, "Drunk again, sis? How many times do I need to come to your rescue? Get your addictions under control. You're a grown woman! Next time, I'm just leaving you there. You must really think I have nothing better to do than carry you home. Wait until your husband hears about *this* one! I'm sure he's going to throw a fit!"

He had pretended enough what it would be like to have a family, and this was one of the scenarios he had invented in his mind. It seemed to work like a charm. Some people looked at him weird; others kind of chuckled with an acknowledging grin, as if to say, "Yep, we've all been there."

"Not here you haven't," he thought as he kept walking.

They approached his apartment, and he opened the door. He never locked it. Zach would've welcomed the opportunity of someone breaking into his home, but no one ever had.

He plopped her unresponsive body onto the couch and just stared at her. Then he bound her hands and feet with some rope, ensuring she wouldn't go anywhere once she woke up.

While waiting for her to gain consciousness, he fixed himself a virgin cocktail. He had alcohol in the house but never drank the stuff. For what he did, he needed to stay clean. Besides, he didn't want to wind up like his dearly departed guardian, Joe. The alcohol was just a reminder of what he'd been through and why he was the way he was. It kept him going without ever taking a sip.

Sleeping beauty began to come out of her induced trance, and Zach made sure to be standing over her when she opened her pretty eyes. He didn't stuff anything in her mouth to gag her. He wanted her to be able to answer his questions.

"Good morning, beautiful," he said, smiling.

She stared at him with obvious terror flashing in her eyes.

"Do you know why you're lying on *my* couch?"

"Please," she begged. "My husband has money. He'll give you whatever you need; just let me go. I'm sure he's looking for me by now. He knows where I went, so he's probably right outside your door; not far from it anyway. My name is Darla."

She had read somewhere that humanizing yourself might trigger your captor to realize the intensity of what he or she was doing, but it didn't help her in this case. He just kept repeating her name, almost as if it gave him more ammunition against her.

"Really, Darla? Do you even know where you are? You've been asleep for an hour. We could be in Arizona. Are you sure he's outside *my* door?" With that he opened his door, pretending to look for him. She opened her mouth to scream, and he shut the door.

"You can scream if you want to, but then I have to gag you. Is that what you want, Darla? I *am* here to please, after all." He held a rag, spinning it around so it would become tight enough to slip in her mouth and tie around her head to gag her. He was about to walk toward her.

"Now, I opened up that door, but ya see, no husband was there waiting for you. He must have gotten over you already. Poor Darla. I'd bet that he was just sick of your bitchy ways and has already moved on to the next pretty girl."

As scared as she was, she was starting to get pissed off. He was toying with her, and that was something she was definitely *not* used to. "You can't hurt me. Look at you; you're what, eighteen? You're just another useless punk. Is this how you teenagers get your kicks these days? Let me tell you something, I go to the gym *every* day. I can defend myself in a heartbeat. If you think I'm scared, think again."

Zach just laughed at this statement and stared at his hostage. In a flash, he suddenly grew serious and grim. He jumped up from his seat and crouched down next to her, bringing his face in close to hers and watching her eyes as they widened in horror.

In a gruff voice, barely audible, he let her know exactly how he felt. "Defend yourself, ma'am? I'm sorry, Darla, but you seem to forget. Who seems to be tied up at the moment?" He wiggled his hands in front of her as if to prove to her that he was the one who was free. "I'm sorry to be the one to tell you this, but as you can see, no one else is here. You can try to defend yourself all you want. I have no problem with that, but nothing you do will help get you out of the predicament you put yourself in."

He could sometimes feel a small bit of empathy for most of his victims, stemming from the fact that he was a victim as well. This woman, however, received no such sentiment from him. She was someone who perceived herself to be invincible and above everyone else. His job this evening was to prove otherwise. He looked out the window—complete darkness mixed with a rare desert thunderstorm. Perfect. He smiled at her one last time and then started to put the gag in her mouth. "Anything you want to say?"

She was now reduced to groveling. "Please, *please*. What do you want?"

"I want to be somebody else. Unfortunately, I don't think you can help me with that, Darla." With that, he stuffed the rag in her mouth and carried her out to the back seat of the car. The drive to the remote area where he dumped all of his victims took about thirty minutes. The walk to seclusion took about another thirty.

As he drove, he switched on the radio and talked to his victim as if she were a passenger in a taxi cab. "Lovely evening, isn't it? Barely rains here, but when it does, the whole city seems to just glisten before us. Have you noticed that? Do you like jazz?" he asked, turning the radio up a little. "I do. It calms me."

She sat wide-eyed in the backseat, allowing her eyes to adjust to the dark. The thunderous beating of her heart was in synch with the pouring rain that pounded the car's hood. Darla tried to focus on anything that could help her, something she could use to bash him over the head. She didn't care if the car crashed, as it was possible to survive that, but her intelligence told her she wouldn't survive at the hands of this man. Nothing. The backseat was spotless.

"We have a long night ahead of us. Of course, not really you. More me. You'll be pretty relaxed, I must say. It's me who has to do all the work. Don't worry; I'm not the type to rape you first or anything sick like that. I'm not saying you have a disease or anything. I just don't like to play Russian roulette. You're not my type anyway. Someone should've given you an attitude adjustment years ago. If they had, you wouldn't be caught up in this quandary tonight."

As she listened to him ramble on, she tried desperately to remove the rope.

"No use longing for the past though; however, your rude ways define who you are. My intolerance for bitchiness defines me. I guess opposites do attract. It's true what they say." He looked in his rearview mirror and, just as he thought, little Miss Bitch had been reduced to tears.

"Had you smiled back at me, your night would've been drastically different. I was just looking for some friendliness. A guy can get lonely, you know. Sometimes a smile can brighten one's day. I think I read that on a bumper sticker once. If not, maybe I should market that. What do you think? Come on, Darla. It may actually save lives! Work with me here!"

He laughed at this. "If I were the type to leave a signature, I'd draw a smiley face on you. But the truth is, I don't leave signatures. I change my MO based on how I feel at that precise moment, and I don't take souvenirs. I did take your money. Sorry, but you won't need that. But that's all I took. I promise."

She looked down and saw that he wasn't lying. She still had her gaudy, princess-cut diamond ring wrapped around her finger and felt her expensive gold necklace roped around her neck.

She couldn't be sure, but it felt like her earrings were still intact. The jewelry she wore wasn't her best but was still worth at least twenty thousand dollars, and he didn't take a thing.

She would've never walked on the street alone wearing all of this jewelry if it were not for her car getting a flat tire and her cell phone losing its signal. She was nervous about getting robbed, but never about being killed! Did he truly just want a smile? Had she really induced the end of her life by not smiling at a stranger?

"We're almost there now. Just about fifteen minutes left. I know you can't wait." He reached over to open his glove compartment and scrambled through the items in there until he found what he was looking for.

He caught the woman trying to see what he was grasping and put her out of her misery. "Oh, this old thing? This is a knife. I used to use it when I went fishing at the lake in Arizona. It was great to scale a fish with. You look surprised; murderers *do* other stuff other than murder.

"But you're right. I don't fish much anymore. I never really liked it. That was all a half-hearted attempt to be human. As you can see, it didn't work out too well.

He spoke in a very matter-of-fact manner, which only frightened Darla more.

"Instead, I'm going to use this to puncture your heart. If you behave, I'll make it quick and painless. The blood won't even spatter too much if I stop your heart in one quick thrust.

"See, the heart is the muscle that pumps blood through the body," he explained as if he were a biology teacher giving a lesson. "If you stop the muscle before it can pump anymore, it's a nice, clean kill. If you move around too much, however, I'm afraid it'll be a bit messier and probably a lot more painful." He shrugged. "It's your choice."

She pressed her eyes together and did her best not to cry. She had to get out of this. There had to be a way. She could sweet-talk her way out of any mess, but she was gagged. *Think, Darla, think!*

They drove a few more miles before he pulled to the side of the road and killed the engine. He put his hand behind the headrest of the passenger seat and looked in the backseat at the struggling woman.

"Just a smile. A beautiful woman like you couldn't give me just that?" He paused as though expecting a reply. "OK. Are you ready, *Darrrlaaa*?" He dragged out her name like he was asking a puppy if he wanted to go on an evening walk.

He carried her out of the car and gently lowered her to the ground. She tried to put up a fight, squirming and screaming through her gag. With what little mobility she had, she tried to kick and crawl, but it was of no use. She wasn't going anywhere.

He bent down to be at eye level with her and touched her face. Zach didn't want to hover over her. He didn't have the God complex so many other killers did. He didn't feel superior to anyone. He wanted to be at her level.

Her eyes pleaded with him, and he understood. It didn't change his mind though. "Don't worry. It'll be over before you know it. Unless, of course, you want me to drag it out a little. I can do that too. I bet this is the most excitement a spoiled, rich housewife like you has come across in a while. I'm an easygoing guy, or, as you like to say, a useless punk."

Though she couldn't speak, he gazed at her for a moment for a reaction—like he could read her mind.

"I know what you're asking me, and I regret to inform you that once my mind is made up, there's nothing you can do to change it."

In an instant he pounced to a standing position, bent at the waist, and stared directly into her eyes. He held her face in his left hand, shook his head in a sympathetic manner, and gently stroked her cheek. She tried to nestle her face against him, again pleading for recourse by acting submissive, but he was unaffected.

He pulled his right arm back and, with one swift motion, thrust the knife deep through her heart. As she slumped forward onto the ground, he gazed up toward the starlit sky and let the rain cover his face and hair. He was right. Except for a few droplets of blood, the kill was clean—quick and painless.

After a moment of peace, he bent at his knees and draped the lifeless body over his shoulder once again. This time, she had moved on out of this world. Before rigor mortis set in, he positioned her mouth upward on both sides, giving himself the one thing he had wanted—just a simple smile.

Chapter 31

Amber gasped for breath as she awoke from her dream. It was 3:00 a.m. Her throat felt raw, as if she hadn't had a beverage in days.

"Amber," her mother said, standing at the foot of her bed. "What's wrong? You were screaming. You ok?" Her mom's eyes showed concern.

Amber still felt disoriented. The room looked fuzzy, and she could barely make out the shadow that she soon recognized to be her mom.

"Amber!"

"Mom," she whispered as she struggled to get her voice back. "I'm fine. I just had a weird dream. That's all. Really, go back to bed."

"Honey, you were *screaming* out of control!"

"It was *just* a bad dream. I'll talk to you in the morning."

Alex saw that her daughter was OK, left the room, and went back to her own bedroom—the same one she used to share with her husband and where she used to rock both Amber and Kevin to sleep.

She wondered if she had made the wrong decision in not telling Amber she'd once had a beautiful brother. She knew hiding him was wrong, but if Kevin was dead, why should Amber need to mourn two people before she was even two years old? No, it was the right decision.

With counseling, Amber would come to accept the circumstances surrounding her father's murder and live a normal, happy life. She seemed to be adjusting well during the awkward, rebellious teenage years and, come to think of it, hadn't tried to rebel even once.

Wide awake now, Alex missed Jack and Kevin more than ever. It had been fourteen years since she'd felt her husband's touch or rocked her baby to sleep. She got up and walked to the closet where she still had some of Jack's love letters and began sifting through them one by one.

Before she knew it, it was 7:00 a.m. With tear-stained cheeks, she decided it was time to officially get up. Folding the last letter neatly back into its faded envelope, Alex put her husband's belongings away and went into the shower.

When she got dressed and came downstairs, she found Amber eating cereal at the kitchen table overlooking their huge yard.

"Morning, Mom."

"Morning, honey. How're you feeling?"

"Me? I'm fine. You look a little like shit though, Mom, if you don't mind me saying so. Your eyes are bright red. Bloodshot, like you've been crying. Are you OK?"

Other than the life-altering lie of Amber not having a dead brother, Alex had never lied to Amber, as though not lying to her ever again would make up for that one major one.

"I'm fine, sweetheart. Just thinking of your father. I wish he were here to see how you've grown up. He would've been so proud. I miss him." She lowered her head and wiped her tears away. "Enough of that. What's on the agenda for today? Going to Tiffany's?"

"Probably. We wanted to go bowling this afternoon."

"Sure. That's a good idea. I can drive you."

"Mom, did Dad have any siblings?"

"No. He was an only child."

"Did you and he want to have more children?"

Alex shuddered at this question and wrapped her arms around herself. She'd never had to answer any questions like that before. She just never told Amber about Kevin, and Amber never knew to ask.

"We thought about it, but, it just didn't happen in time." She choked back tears once again as she said this but figured she covered it up well enough.

Amber looked at her mom and knew she was hurting. "I'm sorry, Mom. I wish I knew Dad. I know how much you miss him. I hope I'm not being insensitive when I ask about him. Sometimes I'm just curious, ya know?"

"It's fine, Amber. What time do you and Tiffany want to go bowling?"

"Let me call her now. I'll let you know."

Just then, the phone rang. It was Tiffany, and Amber was happy to hear from her. "How about I just come over now, and we can go bowling later? Sound OK?"

"Sure!" Amber said. "Come over."

Tiffany only lived four blocks away—a fifteen-minute walk.

Within minutes, Amber greeted Tiffany as she was walked up the driveway. "I'm so glad you're here. Come on in," she whispered. "I'm going nuts! I know you're going to think I'm crazy, but I had another psychotic dream last night, and apparently I was screaming like a lunatic. My mother came in!"

"Oh, no. She probably thinks you're going to need counseling again."

"I don't know, Tiff. She might be right. This one was really extreme. So lifelike and not poetic like the others, as you had so ingeniously labeled them."

Tiffany sat down on the edge of Amber's bed as Amber shut the door. "Should I get some popcorn for this?"

"Tiffany, I'm serious! I can't focus on anything else. I tried to make some ordinary conversation with my mom, but all I could talk about was my father. I think I made her even more upset. This dream was so *real.*"

"Well, let's hear it. I'm going to have to start charging you, though, ya know. The going rates for dream analysts aren't cheap by any means," Tiffany said, smirking .

"OK, well, I'll have to remember that. Just consider me having to hang out with you as payment enough," Amber said. She took a deep breath. "OK, I hope I can recall the whole thing, but I don't foresee myself having any problem. Here goes. We were walking in the desert, of all places. Probably somewhere like Las Vegas or Arizona. It seemed like it was snowing. There were white mounds the size of cars throughout the valley, except it wasn't snow; it was sand. I think it was sand anyway.

"We came across this old, stucco house and met an elderly couple that owned it. The house had to be at least fifty years old, if not more. They seemed nice enough but were kind of standoffish. Like you," she chided. Amber had a habit of making jokes when she was truly scared or hurting. It was a defense mechanism she had mastered when she was young.

"They had a son, I guess. Sort of good looking, but in a scruffy kind of way. I felt like I knew him but don't know from where. I do know it's the same face as the boy in my other dreams. Even now, as I'm telling you, he's still haunting me, but in a weird, comforting type of way.

"Anyhow, we met them and continued on our walk. Then after a little while, we turned back. I noticed that house had some of the biggest snow/sand banks out of all of the houses on the block.

She noticed Tiffany smirking. "Just listen to the rest of it, okay?"

"Oh, I'm listening. I'm a little scared of you, but I'm listening," she teased.

Amber rolled her eyes and continued on. "By the back gate were a few kittens. They looked hungry. Maybe even starved. Beside them sat a bowl of sour milk mixed with what looked like dirt. The kittens were covered with mud and were so filthy.

"Again, here you were in the dream with me, forcing your way into the backyard. You said we had a right to rescue all of these kittens."

"Sure, I can see myself saying that."

Ignoring her friend, Amber continued on. "I tended to agree with you, as I always seem to do, but had to lean against something as I felt like I was going to pass out. I decided to lean against that snow/sand bank. I still didn't know what it was. It was very cold, so it could've been snow, but it was too much snow to accumulate in the desert. But, hey, I guess it *is* my dream, right?

"So, I leaned on this thing and felt something hard underneath. It was a different texture than the snow bank. I turned to look at it, and as I did, you had just lifted up a kitten. The kitten meowed, at the same time that I turned around and realized of what I was leaning on."

"What was it?" Tiffany asked, now intrigued.

"Piles of rotting flesh, and facing up was a dead woman! She looked like she'd just been killed. I remember looking at the house and trying to imagine how their neighbors couldn't have noticed a dead body, and only then did I realize that there was more than just one. There were dozens! Bones, flesh—some rotted, some still intact.

"It was like being in the middle of a graveyard in which the bodies had no coffins. And, oh yeah, they weren't buried! I tried to tell some of the other neighbors, and they warned me to stay away and pretend I didn't see anything. It was so disturbing. I think it was at that point that I must've screamed and woke up, and that's when my mother came running in."

Tiffany looked concerned. "Have you ever considered seriously going for counseling? I mean, I'm not trying to be funny. Maybe these dreams are trying to tell you something that you're afraid to face in real life. Know what I mean? It might be worth a shot. If not, hell, you can always make a movie out of them. They are sick enough, in a pretty cool kind of way."

"Tiffany, you're no help." Amber pretended to be mad, but Tiffany was just doing what she did best—make people laugh. "I'll remember if I'm ever feeling blue to make sure I don't call you. There's gotta be some meaning in these dreams. Once I fell back asleep, another nightmare came haunting me. Two in one night! Am I ever going to get sleep?"

Tiffany nodded sympathetically, prompting Amber to go on.

"The other dream was about a really pretty woman, maybe mid-twenties, about to get murdered. Her killer threatened that he was going to stab her. They were located outside by a cave or something like that. It was really dark, and her killer spoke to her in a soothing voice. She looked terrified, like she had begged and begged, but her life was still coming to an end.

"Her eyes were desperate and pleading, but the killer was that *same* person, once again, who is in all of my dreams. Somehow I got the vibe that he felt nothing at all. I guess to kill someone, you'd have to feel that way. It was eerie and scared me to death. I actually heard her heart pumping in my dream, until he pulled back the knife and I saw him stab her! It was all too visual and all too real.

"I feel like, 'Am I that messed up in the head, where I can't even have one peaceful night's sleep without dreaming about people getting killed or dead bodies floating around?'"

"Well, we do watch a ton of scary movies. I think that, coupled with..."

"Go ahead. Say it, Tiff. I'm not going to forget that he's gone. That coupled with the brutal murder of my father..." Amber let her sentence trail off.

"Sorry. Yes, that. Those two things alone are reason enough for you to have these freaky, horror-movie-type dreams. Perhaps we should stick to love stories and cartoons. Maybe you'll dream you were swept away by a prince with a beautiful car and an amazing mansion."

"Yeah, right. With my luck, it would wind up being one of the cartoon characters sweeping me off of my feet. Besides, shouldn't a prince drive up in a horse and carriage? I think I'd rather have the scary dreams."

"Listen, let's find out what time the bowling alley opens. We can get dropped off there, go bowling, and hit a diner or that Chinese restaurant afterward. Let's make a day of it, maybe go the mall too. What do you think?"

"Sounds good," Amber said. "Let me check and see what my mom's doing. I think she said she can drive us today."

Alex sat in her bedroom, trying to pull herself together. In just a few short years, she'd gone from having the most incredible life to losing both her husband and son. Now she felt as if she was losing her mind as well. The guilt of not telling Amber she had a twin brother weighed on her more than ever.

Amber walked in the room, snapping her out of her trance. "Mom, can you drive us to the bowling alley? It's right on Main Street. You mind?"

"Sure, honey. Let me get my keys. Hi, Tiff."

"Hi, Mrs. Rider. Thanks for taking us."

Alex was glad at least that Tiffany was there for Amber. They'd met a few years earlier in school and had been inseparable ever since. It was great that they were such good friends and had always looked out for each other. Tiffany was an only child, so they were as much like sisters as they could be. Alex was ecstatic that Amber had someone to trust and confide in.

Chapter 32

Last night's kill was somewhat satisfying to Zach, though it still left something more to be desired. He was getting better and quicker each time. The walk to his secluded spot, however, was becoming more of a hassle.

The summer months were approaching, and in the desert, the temperature could easily hit one hundred and fifteen degrees during the day. To his advantage, Zach only liked to go out at night, but it wasn't much cooler then. Maybe only ninety after the sun finally set.

The walk was a long one. Two miles of carrying literal dead weight wasn't easy by any means. In the corner of his mind, Zach contemplated getting a wagon. One of those little Radio Flyer wagons he'd never had the luxury of owning. Perhaps he could live out that part of his childhood now. However, he didn't think it was intended for transporting dead bodies.

It would never make it over the uneven, rocky terrain, but he could attach a mountain bike to it and then sort of drive his "passengers" up there. Though it was more of a juvenile thought, he did think it through and even considered it a bit before deciding against it. He imagined himself getting caught and how ridiculous he would look riding a bike, trailing a wagon with a dead body hanging loosely over the sides. Nah. He would continue killing as he had been. It seemed to work fine for him.

His hunger for killing was usually sated after just one kill. For some reason, however, this one just didn't suffice. He didn't want to get greedy since this one was taken so close to home, but he'd have to do it soon.

He was feeling a little bit of self-pity about the life he was given and wondered why he was even born into this world. Was it to kill the bitchy women? How about the rude men? Even Zach knew it wasn't morally correct to just kill because he didn't like someone's attitude, but those were the most fun.

Unlike a vigilante killer, he didn't kill just because people were bad. He killed for the mere reason that some people were bad to *him*. He didn't care about their personal lives—whether the victim was a murderer or sang in the church choir. He only killed to satisfy his own personal, selfish needs. No one else's even came into play. If the person was nice to him and showed him respect, they got to live another day. Simple.

Since he'd spent last night in the caves, he decided to make the walk back to his car and drive home. He would then eat some breakfast and sleep for the remainder of the scorching hot day. Once nighttime fell upon the city, he would decide if there would be a murder on the hidden streets of Las Vegas. This time, he would have to be a bit more careful. Two murders in two days, and the police would get suspicious.

As nighttime approached, Zach got up and stretched. He took some leftover meat from his hunting expedition in the mountains out of the mini-fridge and started to cook the coyote. Once finished with dinner, he sat on the comfortable old leather couch, deciding what to do with the possibilities that lie before him.

If he was going to The Strip, he would have to at least look presentable. Instead, he figured he would go downtown. It wasn't as nice, and people seemed to notice you less around there. Everyone was either looking for their next hit of crack or just a sip of alcohol. It was nowhere near as ritzy as The Strip, and that was more his style.

He showered and even had to shave a bit. At fifteen, just a bit of peach fuzz was starting to come in. No one had ever taught how to shave; he just sort of winged it. He thought he looked good.

He got in his old but reliable car and headed down the freeway toward downtown Las Vegas. He parked his car on one of the side roads instead of parking it in the old parking garage—privacy was essential. He began walking around under the canopy of lights and took notice of all the different types of people who frequented the casinos. While seeking out his next victim, he did enjoy some time to people watch.

Some were families, and he wondered why their young children were hanging out in a casino. Some were men with their pants hanging well below their waistline, almost reaching their knees. He shook his head in disgust and wondered why the hell they would wear them out like that. Did they not realize how ridiculous they looked? He almost singled out one of them as his victim for the mere fact that he didn't want to look at the guy's ass hanging out of his jeans any longer, and maybe this would make a statement to the rest of those followers sporting the new fashion.

He looked at a boy about his age hanging out with his parents. They were talking about school, joking around, laughing, and seemed to be having a good time. His father had his arm draped around the boy's shoulder and playfully punched him in the stomach. They all just laughed a little more and continued walking while taking in the lights, glitter, and enticing shops on the side and middle of the road. No cars were allowed down there, as it was made specifically just for walking.

Zach grew more and more jealous as he watched the teen and his family, which made him feel more out of control. The only thing that made him feel *in* control was killing.

Just as that thought crossed his mind, a drunk, vagrant man, around the same age that Joe was when he met his unfortunate demise, bumped into Zach. Then, instead of apologizing, he just laughed and actually had the audacity to flick the hat off of Zach's head.

Without even turning back, the drunk just kept staggering down the block, bumping into people and inanimate objects as he passed. He mumbled something to himself and would occasionally give a big, toothy grin, displaying the three teeth he had left—most likely due to some type of drug, possibly meth.

Zach bent down to pick up his hat and leisurely followed the man. Luckily for him, the man was headed in the direction of his car. This was going to be easier than he thought. Zach didn't even need to run to catch up. The man was too drunk to be walking at any more than a snail's pace.

Within three seconds of seeing this vagrant, he already had formulated a foolproof plan. He stayed close behind, and when it seemed the man was about to change direction, Zach made his move. This was one of the perks to wearing crappy clothes out.

"Hey man. Wanna party?" Zach asked.

The drunk mumbled something indistinct and kept staggering on his way but seemed to be having a bit of trouble keeping his balance.

"Whoa, big fella! Let me help you there," Zach said, reaching out to steady him. "Had too much to drink, huh? Happens to me more times than I like to admit," he lied. "I have a little crack pipe that I can share with you. Might make you feel a whole lot better. My only condition is that you just have to remember to return the favor when I'm out of the stuff. Sound like a plan?"

"You a cop?" he mumbled, not quite pronouncing the "p" in cop, but Zach understood what he was getting at.

"Do I look like a cop, man? Hell, no. I just got a little extra tonight, and you seem like just the type of man who could use some. My car isn't far from here. Not a fancy ride or anything, but it runs. You can lean on me if you need to. I see you're having a bit of trouble walking."

He helped the guy into the backseat of the car. "There's some extra room back here for you to relax. We'll be at my place in no time."

Zach drove for forty-five minutes to his personal graveyard. He didn't have to do a thing to restrain Mr. Drunk, who was passed out cold in the backseat. Zach could have easily killed him with one blow, but he wanted the man to be awake and sober so he knew exactly why his life was ending at this precise point in time.

Zach checked the guy's wallet for money, and to his surprise, the man still had ten dollars. He probably had just stolen it from some poor, unsuspecting tourist downtown. This was plenty. He was getting kind of hungry, so before arriving at his destination, he pulled into a fast-food drive-through and ordered a double cheeseburger, large fries, and a chocolate shake. He didn't usually have an appetite like this, but it could be hours before his "friend" woke up. He had to keep his own energy up to be awake and fully ready for the kill.

After paying the cashier and getting his food, Zach continued on until he reached his spot. He pulled over and put the radio on. Today he was in the mood for some rock 'n' roll, instead of his usual jazz station. A popular heavy metal band came on the radio, the front man singing about how life sucked and he was going to kill everyone.

"I know how you feel man. I'm with ya," Zach said. He downed his burger in about three quick bites and scavenged his fries just as quickly. He savored the shake and made it last a while. Just as he finished his last gulp, his passenger began to stir in the backseat.

"Hey, good morning. How did you sleep?"

The drunk was now fully awake and started to try and remember where he was. He didn't have the typical hangover. He was so used to being drunk that he rarely got a headache, and if he did, he just was going to start drinking again anyway. "Where are we? Didn't you say you had some crack?"

"Oh, I did. But you know, you passed out, so I smoked it all by myself."

"That's messed up. Where are we?"

"Oh, we're just hanging out listening to rock and roll. I'm glad you're awake. I thought I wouldn't see you until morning, and I'm more of a night owl. I would've had to wake you for the occasion."

"What occasion?"

"Come outside with me," Zach said cheerfully. "I really don't like to show people my surprises inside the car."

"No, man," the bum said, shaking his head. "Take me back downtown. I don't like this. Where the hell are we? Looks like we're in the middle of fuckin' nowhere."

"I thought you were going to act rationally. This is all wrong. You need to do as I say. It's getting late. If you didn't sleep so damn much, I wouldn't have to rush this."

The guy went to hit Zach over the head, but he soon realized his hands were bound together. As he looked further, he saw that his feet were bound as well. "What the hell? You some sick son of a bitch or something? I don't go that way, if that's what you're thinking. Untie me!"

"Now, now. Is that the way you think you should speak to me? Do you know why you're here?"

"Yes. Because you're one sick son of a bitch!"

"Well, that argument remains to be seen. See, I never had a mother. Not one that I actually knew anyway, so I do not know if she was a bitch or not. And I'm not really sick. Actually, I have never felt healthier in my entire life. No, that answer was wrong.

"I'm not a sick son-of-a-bitch. I'm just the guy who you bumped into and decided to make matters worse by not only your lack of apology, but you decided to take it a step further and purposely knock my hat right off of my head. You even laughed about it, didn't you? So, let's share a good laugh about that now. What do ya say?" Zach said with a big, malevolent belly laugh.

"Not so funny anymore, is it? Think you can manage a chuckle for me now, you toothless drunk?"

"Untie me! I got some good cocaine back at my apartment. It's all yours."

"Thanks pal, but I don't do drugs. Giving me cocaine is like giving filet mignon to a vegetarian. Nah, I just wanted to let you know that your inability to apologize and your rude behavior is what brought you to your inescapable demise."

Zach reached for a hammer this time. He was still feeling inadequate in his own life and needed to get his anger out in some way. He dragged the man out of the backseat and let him fall to the ground in a fetal position. He lifted the hammer high above his own head, all the while listening to the man beg continuously for what he considered to be his precious life.

In one swift motion, Zach brought the hammer down on the man's skull. He managed to survive the first blow and attempted to crawl away, but after that, Zach took his pathetic life from him within minutes. This wasn't as clean a kill as the woman, but Zach needed a bit more violence than he had yesterday.

Blood had splattered all over him. It was a good thing he always kept a change of clothes in the trunk. He brought the bag of clothes along with the bleeding man to the very spot where he disposed of all of his bodies and once again was too tired to make the drive home.

After throwing the body in a prime feeding spot for wildlife, Zach changed into his new clothes, lit a fire on top of some rocks, and burned his and the man's clothes. It was a bit cooler out in the desert tonight, so he was confident that the fire would burn out on its own. He then made himself comfortable in the confines of a small cave, ready to take a small nap, walk back to his car, and then drive home before sunrise.

Chapter 33

Zach began his two-mile hike back to the start of civilization, where he always hid his car behind an old, abandoned building. No one ever went back there. He knew this because he has scouted out the area himself for two months, day after day, to make sure this would be the perfect location for his killings and burials. He was certain it was secluded.

As he approached his car, he realized he'd made a grave mistake. Two men were walking toward it. This wasn't good. If they got close enough, they might see the blood stains he'd left on the sandy gravel beneath it. What the hell were people doing here anyway?

He hadn't had the time or energy to clean it up last night. He thought it could wait until morning. If he needed to, he could make a quick getaway. His car had false license plates on it, so all he needed to do was get home, throw them out, and steal some new ones. It's not like it was registered in his name, or anyone's name for that matter. He just always drove carefully to be sure not to get pulled over.

He tried to get to the people fast enough to distract them from seeing the blood. "Hey guys; how's it going? Seems like it's going to be another hot day here in the valley, doesn't it?"

"Sure does. Is this your car?"

"Yep, that's mine. Not much of anything, but it gets me where I need to go."

They saw it. He noticed them looking at him and then back at the car, their eyes focusing on the black liquid pooled beneath it.

"You have an accident or something? There's an awful amount of what looks like blood over there, right outside the passenger side of your car."

He could kill them both right now. He thought about it. He hadn't prepared for it, and truthfully, he didn't know if he possessed the energy. Last night's kill had taken a lot out of him, and he hadn't eaten or had anything to drink in over eight hours. He needed to think fast.

"Yeah, I thought the same thing. It kind of looks like motor oil, though I didn't want to get too close to find out. Thought it might be an injured animal. I'm quite the nature lover, so I took a walk back through the desert to see if I could help. I walked about a quarter of a mile, but I got kind of tired. It's all uphill. Not an easy hike if you're not used to it. I'm sure it's nothing, or if it was something, the coyotes probably got to it by now. What are you guys doing all the way out here anyway?"

"Us? We're from the county's office. Needed to take a look at this building here. They're thinking of knocking it down. It's just taking up space being out here on an open road. They may eventually want to put a casino out here, so we're getting the specifications just in case we need it for zoning. Just what Las Vegas needs, right? Another casino? How about you? Kind of a lonely road for a teenager to be going for an early morning stroll, isn't it?"

They know. The small guy on the left kept staring at the blood stain and then back at Zach. Zach was getting paranoid too. He didn't remember if he'd wiped any blood off of his face. He touched his chin to try and feel for any tell-tale signs.

"I never come this way; just passing through. But, my luck, got a flat. It's all fixed now, though. It could have been worse. The engine on that old thing could have quit on me. "I have no cell phone either. I would've been stuck out here all day. Well, if I hadn't run into y'all." He spoke to them in a Texas drawl, just in case they ever needed to identify him to the police.

"Well, I better get going. Nice talking to you, gentlemen." Zach had no clue where he'd developed his charm, but it seemed to be the one thing he had going for him.

As he started his short drive home, Zach thought about the men he had just met. They seemed clueless, but the one man seemed to have a bit more of an interest in things that didn't concern him. He'd have to remember that if he ever ran into him alone in a dark alley.

The men didn't look fit enough to walk two miles up hill on the rocky terrain, but if they did, they would be in for quite a surprise. The decomposing remains were well hidden in the back of a deep cave, underneath piles and piles of tumbleweed and dried up leaves.

It wasn't something that could be easily stumbled upon—unless, of course, a coyote pup dug it up and used it as a chew toy. That was a definite possibility, but Zach was going to have to rely upon fate that no evidence would be found.

Zach decided to lose the license plates nearby and steal new ones from the other side of town. Daylight was approaching quickly, and he just wanted to get home. It was time to wash up, take a good snooze, and see what the rest of the day had in store.

Generally, Zach could go home, eat breakfast, and then sleep until the sun went down without any issues. A few days per month, he found that he couldn't sleep. It didn't happen often, but when it did, it didn't bother him much. He didn't own a television and couldn't remember the last time he had actually watched a show or a movie. Usually when he couldn't sleep, he lied down on his old couch and got absorbed in a good book.

Reading was the one outlet Zach had from his lonely, pathetic life. It was the one *good* thing Joe had taught him. Without reading, he would have nothing. The books he got were free, as he borrowed them from the public library by using a fake ID he had created for such occasions. He would not stoop to stealing books.

Ironically, the only true crime Zach committed was a little murder now and then. Other than that, he considered himself a pretty decent citizen. He didn't steal (from the living anyway), and he even helped an old lady cross the street one day. He wouldn't kill children or the elderly. He prided himself on reading at least two books every week. They knew him well at the library and were actually nice to him.

He almost enjoyed the times he couldn't sleep so he could get caught up on a good read and forget the life he had to live through.

Today was probably going to be one of those days. He was too preoccupied with the man who kept staring at him and was a little nervous that they would catch on to his dirty little secret.

Once he grew tired of reading, he'd begin planning the rest of his evening. He did not feel any immediate need to kill. For now, the hunger had subsided and he felt satisfied. That could change within a few hours; however, he didn't think it would tonight.

As he lay down, he clasped his hands behind his head and revisited the past two nights' kills, opened his book, and began reading. After about one hundred pages, he closed his eyes, dreamt of a girl he recognized but didn't know, and didn't wake up until the next morning.

Chapter 34

Tiffany and Amber were having a blast at the bowling alley. Neither of them were considered good bowlers by any means, but they were decent enough to get by. Amber was having fun modeling her rented bowling shoes. "They could at least make them somewhat stylish," she joked.

"Oh, I don't know. They look kind of nice to me. I don't think I'll go out and buy a pair right now, but who knows? We *are* going to the mall later."

"Oh, definitely!"

Amber got a spare on her first try, and Tiffany knocked a whopping three pins down. Amber was going for the strike on her second turn, but luck wasn't with her. Neither was skill for that matter. As she missed the last pin, they both jumped up and down like she'd won a gold medal and started giggling, as they always did.

They played a total of three games, and by the time they were done, they were starved. They skipped their plan to go to the mall and instead went right next door to a Chinese restaurant that was inexpensive enough for them to afford. They started talking a little more seriously over dinner, and Amber started to open up.

"Sometimes, I feel like I'm crazy. I mean, I know I told you about the dreams, and they are freaky enough, but like you pointed out, they *are* just dreams.

"But sometimes it's a little more than that. I know we joke about me going to counseling, but the more I think about it, the more I think it may not be such a bad idea.

"The dreams disturb me enough, but I also have these uncontrollable feelings like there's something more; something I'm missing."

"Like what?"

"See, I know my father dying—well, getting murdered—is a huge part of it. It bothers me that they never found the guy and that they really didn't know much about his motive.

"From what I hear, the guy sort of snapped, killed his boyfriend's ex-boyfriend, and then killed his boyfriend. Then, of course, a few months later, my father became the target of his anger, and my mother was almost killed as well.

"Did you know she had bullet wounds in her arm and stomach?"

"Yeah, I remember you telling me that. Unbelievable!"

"The doctors say it's a miracle that it didn't hit any major organs. Apparently I was upstairs in my crib, so I didn't get hurt and didn't even hear a sound.

"What disturbs me, though, is that this guy, Steve, worked with my father for over ten years, and they never had any type of fight. I guess apparently he'd lost his mind and went on secret killing binges whenever things didn't go his way.

"I have just always felt like there was something weird about the whole story. It feels like whenever the topic comes up about my father, everyone kind of exchanges glances and repeats the same story, but then changes the topic in a subtle kind of way."

"What else can there be, though?" Tiffany asked. "They told you probably the worst news any daughter can hear about her father. It's not like they sugarcoated *that*. That story in itself is pretty harsh, Amber. I'm sure they've told you all there is to know. I'd imagine talking about that night brings up horrible memories and was such a traumatic experience. Have you ever thought that maybe it's just *really* difficult to speak about?"

Just as they started to get deep into their conversation, their food came. Amber ordered her usual—chicken and broccoli. Tiffany ordered an egg roll along with sesame chicken. Both of the girls were thin enough; weight was never a problem for them.

"I guess you could be right. It's just…I don't know. There's always a feeling of wanting more. Maybe knowing more information about the man responsible for taking my father's life would help a little. Somehow, I feel like that may help bring some closure to it. It's not like he died of some incurable disease. He was healthy until the second he died."

"Hmm," Tiffany said thoughtfully.

"Hmm what?"

"Well, I was just thinking, if you feel that knowing more about your father's killer may help, ever think of visiting where he used to work? Do you know if that place is still in business? If it is, it wouldn't hurt to go visit there. It's possible that someone still works there that knew both your dad and this asshole, Steve. What do you think?"

"You know what? It's not a terrible idea. It may help even just to hear another side of my father that I'd never heard before and maybe find out some facts about Steve that may help me cope a little better. I should ask my mother if she's ever heard anything about Steve. The last I heard, he was never found, but I haven't asked that question in a long while. I'm going to have to bring that up as well."

They continued eating their dinner while people-watching— pointing and giggling while trying not to get caught. They stayed there for a while enjoying their meals and then cracked open their fortune cookies, adding the phrase "for frogs" at the end of each fortune and laughing like little kids. They opened a few fortune cookies just to add the silly phrase.

"Good luck is coming your way. Make sure you leave the door open...for frogs."

"Mine says: The way to a clear mind is through a mirror...for frogs."

"Hmm. Words to live by." With that, they chuckled and got their money ready to pay the bill. Tiffany called her mother to pick them up. They dropped off Amber, and the girls promised to call each other the next day.

"Hey, Mom," Amber said, walking in the front door.

"Hey! Have a good time with Tiffany? Who won at bowling?"

"I won the first two games. Tiffany won the last game, but not by much. I wouldn't say we're ready to be on national television yet, but give us another few weekends," she joked.

"Have any dinner?"

"Yep. We went to the Chinese restaurant on Main Street near the bowling alley."

"Oh, good. How was it?"

"Delicious, as usual," Amber said, then hesitated before speaking again, trying to think of the right words. "Mom, I have to ask you something. We were talking about Dad during dinner, and I realized that I never knew where he worked. What was the name of the company?"

"Oh, is everything OK? You seem to be talking about him a lot lately."

"Sure. Just thinking of him a bit."

"I'm here if you want to talk, just so you know that. The name of the company was Symmetry, Inc. Your Dad was a computer programmer there, a really good one. But seriously, you OK?"

"I'm fine, Mom. Just thinking lately; that's all. I'm kind of tired, though. I'm going to take a shower and then get ready for bed. I'll come down and say goodnight."

Amber went upstairs and logged onto her computer. She immediately opened up a search engine and typed in "Symmetry Inc., Long Island." It came up on about thirty different citations. Not only was it a popular company, but it was still in business: 3700 Symmetry Way.

Since she didn't drive yet, she would need to take a taxi, but it would have to be during school hours. She started to get butterflies in her stomach and was shaking a little. She was nervous about lying to her mom, but also a little apprehensive about what she would find out. Would anyone there know her father or the man who had brutally killed him? What if her mother found out she'd gone there?

She didn't even know what type of information she was looking for. What would she even say? "*Hi, my father used to work here. He was murdered by someone else who worked here. How do you feel about that?*" Well, that really wasn't going to work, but she would figure it out.

She decided she would go first thing tomorrow and just go to school a little late and forge her mother's signature on the late note. She had no really important classes in the morning. Only one test after lunch, but she should be back by then.

Amber called Tiffany to let her know of her plan and get the green light of approval almost every teenage girl seeks from her best friend at one point or another. Tiffany not only agreed but was excited for her friend, hoping that she could get some closure once and for all.

Chapter 35

The next morning Amber woke up at the crack of dawn, put on her best jeans and semi-dress shirt, and pretended to begin her walk to school as she normally did. She had already called a taxi from her home phone and gave them an address at which to pick her up. She hoped the fare wouldn't exceed ten dollars each way, as she only had twenty-five dollars on her.

As they pulled up to the office building at 8:30 a.m., Amber felt as if her feet were firmly cemented to the interior floor mats of the taxi. She couldn't bring herself to move for a moment, and her heart raced.

"Miss, I believe this is your destination. That'll be eight dollars and fifty cents, please."

"I'm sorry? Oh, OK. Sure." She handed him a ten dollar bill and cautiously stepped out of the cab. "Thank you. Keep the change."

As she approached the glass door, she glanced down at the handle. She wondered if this was the same handle her father had used to open the door every morning upon going into work, then surmised that they had probably installed a new door over the past fourteen years. She looked at the interior of the office as she walked in and wondered where he sat. Where did Steve sit? She expected to feel some type of ghost-like presence upon entering the office, but so far, it was just an ordinary building.

"Hello. May I help you?" the receptionist asked. The name plate on her desk read "Jill Santine."

"Um, well, maybe. My father used to work here, and, um, I...Never mind. I'm sorry to bother you." Amber started to walk out the door.

"No, wait. It's OK. You look familiar. Who was your father?"

Amber thought she'd made a mistake by going there. She felt guilty for lying to her mother, for forging the note, and for skipping school. She was treading on hallowed ground, and felt she should just leave things the way they were. Though she felt she *should* do that, the need was just too great.

"My father was Jack Rider. He was a programmer here many years ago."

"You must be…Wait; don't tell me. It'll come to me. I never forget a name."

Amber's eyes lit up and her knees wobbled. This person may have actually known her father.

"Amber. Is that right?"

"Yes! Did you know my father?"

Jill looked down and to the side of her desk to try and mask her tears. She was still an emotional woman and had been very fond of Jack. She spoke to Amber in an octave just slightly higher than a whisper.

"Yea, I knew him. He was a highly intelligent man. Always helped me out and was very respectable, very funny. He was an honorable man, and you should be proud to have him as your father. I'm so sorry about what happened. No one could've seen it coming. Such a freak thing. All of us went through some self-doubt, being such a bad judge of character with Steve. How old are you now?"

"I'm fifteen. I'm glad you knew him. Everyone sort of tiptoes around the conversation when I bring him up. It's like they think I'll break if I hear his name. Sorry, I don't mean to complain. What was he like, if you don't mind me asking?" She found it extremely easy to talk to Jill. She seemed to have such a warm personality and wondered if her father had thought the same thing.

"Oh, Amber. You would've loved him. Want something to drink? Water? Soda perhaps?"

"No, thank you. I'm fine."

"He was really funny with such a dry sense of humor. He was also charming, but always spoke his mind. Sometimes a little too much for a few people to handle, but I found him hysterical.

"We were all devastated to hear what happened. Steve always seemed like such a nice, quiet man. He didn't bother with anyone much, but never caused a stir either. He even got employee of the month a few times and never made one mistake on the accounting for this company. It was a real shock—a wake-up call, if you know what I mean. You never really know someone. It could've easily been any one of us."

Amber nodded, letting it all sink in.

"Your dad, though. He just adored and loved your mother. Talked about her constantly! Then, when you and…let me think…Kevin were born, he had pictures all over his desk. Couldn't stop bragging, but we didn't mind. He was so proud; it was adorable. Called your mom every day at the same time…"

"Wait, what?"

"Oh, he called every day just to see how you were both doing?"

"What?"

Jill was a little confused at this point. She didn't understand what Amber was questioning. "Amber, is something wrong?"

"Kevin." Amber tried not to seem confused, but was somewhat in a daze, trying to comprehend. She didn't know what Jill was talking about, but she didn't seem to be crazy, and the words were just flowing seamlessly out of her mouth. "I misunderstood the part that you said about *Kevin.*"

Jill looked at Amber with some apprehension but answered her nonetheless. "I was just saying that your dad used to call your mom religiously every day around midmorning to check on you and Kevin. I'm sure it must be difficult."

"Oh, it is. You have no idea how much. I have to get going. It was nice speaking to you. Sorry to have taken up so much of your morning." Amber needed air. She felt like she was going to hyperventilate or vomit—possibly both.

"Wait, Amber. Are you feeling OK?"

"Yes, thank you. I have to go to school. Thank you, Jill."

With a forceful push, she swung open the glass door and sucked in the cool breeze like a fresh burst of oxygen as soon as she walked out. She let the door slam behind her and walked about ten feet—as far as her legs would let her.

She slid down against the cement wall and sat on the concrete, speaking to herself out loud. *Kevin? 'Then, when you and Kevin were born, he had pictures all over his desk.' Is that what she said? When Kevin and I were born? Both of us? Do I have a brother? Do I have a twin brother?* Her head was spinning now.

Could her mother have lied to her? What about her grandparents or her uncle? She was feeling a bit faint and decided to stay put on the ground until she could slow her heart rate down.

She called a taxi from her cell phone. Her next phone call was to her mother at work.

"Mom?"

"Hey, Amber? What's wrong?"

"Mom, can you meet me at the house please?"

"Amber, I have a lot of stuff to do here at work. We're having a big meeting. Can't it wait until I get home?"

"Mom, please?"

"OK. Let me see what I can do. I'll be there as soon as I can." As they hung up, she sighed with frustration. Alex felt very overwhelmed at work, as this was the busiest time of the year. Amber had to pick today of all days to have a teenage crisis. She figured it was due time, as Amber had basically been a good kid, despite all of her misfortunes.

Chapter 36

Amber was sitting in the living room on the recliner staring outside the window at her old swing set, positioned in the corner of the spacious backyard. Her mom walked in shortly after 11:00 a.m., carrying McDonalds for the both of them.

"Thought you might be hungry. OK if we eat while we talk?"

"I'm not hungry, Mom."

"OK. Then *I'm* going to eat while we talk. Since when are you *not* hungry?"

"Mom, I need you to be honest with me, OK?" Amber asked, still staring out the window.

"Of course, but I didn't realize you had to warn me of that first. What's up?"

Amber turned her head and looked her mother straight in the eyes. "Who's Kevin?"

Alex was eating a bite of her cheeseburger and almost choked. She swallowed, put her burger down, nervously wrapped it back up, and stood up. "Amber. Why do you ask?"

"Mom, I asked you to please be honest with me. Who is he?" She was shaking now. Her voice was now trembling, as were her hands.

Now Alex was the one without an appetite. She took a deep breath and held her hands out to Amber. "Honey, please listen to me and let me speak. Let me say what I have to say. Can you do that for me?"

Amber could only nod at this point, swallowing back tears that were fighting to get out. She was terrified about what she was going to hear.

Alex wasn't prepared to have this conversation—not now, not ever. She had never prepared a speech of what she would say or how she would say it because she was hoping to never have to divulge this information.

"Amber, there's no easy way for me to tell you this. Please know that I was trying to make your life a little less painful for you. When you hear what I'm about to tell you, please remember that. Can you do that for me?"

Amber pursed her lips together in annoyance and nodded with some slight hesitation.

"You had a brother; he was your twin. His name was Kevin. He was born seven minutes earlier than you were."

Amber was angrier at her mom now than she had ever been in her whole life. She didn't realize, however, just how angry she would become. She thought that perhaps her brother had died maybe a few days after he was born, maybe SIDS or some horrific, rare disease. She was waiting to hear the tragic story of how he died, never expecting what she was about to learn.

"The night your father was killed, I was shot too, as you well know. What you *don't* know is that you were sleeping like an angel in your crib, but Kevin…" The tears streamed down Alex's face now, and she had to pause. "Kevin was cranky that night. He was asleep in my arms."

"Mom, what are you saying?"

"When I was shot, I was rendered unconscious for two days. When I awoke, they told me that your father had been killed. They then proceeded to tell me that Kevin had been kidnapped by Steve, the same pathetic excuse for a man who killed your father."

Amber just stared at Alex, and Alex got up and started pacing, frantically wiping tears from her eyes and face. "Amber, I just couldn't tell you. I wanted to shield you from any more pain. You already had enough to contend with. I'm so sorry."

Amber's anger turned to sorrow. Not for her mother, not yet anyway. She had a twin that was a year old and was kidnapped by a serial killer.

"Mom, was Kevin's body ever found?"

Alex shook her head. "No, but he's considered dead, honey. The police had no leads. About five years ago, they found Steve's body. He had fallen down a stairwell in some apartment building in North Las Vegas, Nevada. Apparently his alcohol level was almost three times the amount of the legal limit, and he took a nasty spill that ended his life. They said even if he didn't fall, the alcohol poisoning itself was enough to end his life.

"No one there knew who he was, and no child was found with him. They found an ID on him; however, it was a false one bearing the name of Joe Alden. They ran his fingerprints, and they matched up to those of Steve.

"All of the police and child welfare experts said there was a one in a million chance that Kevin was alive. They said he was probably only with Steve a few days before he…disposed of him. I'm so sorry. I wish this wasn't true. It kills me just to get those words out."

"Didn't you ever look for him?"

"Over and over again. I had to go for counseling because I wouldn't stop. I knocked on everyone's door that I could, looking for any signs of Kevin's life. I searched in secluded areas, risking my life late at night to try and find him, but I couldn't. I know you can't forgive me, Amber, but please, please try and understand my reasoning for doing what I did."

For some reason, Amber wasn't angry anymore. She needed some time to think this over and fully grasp what she'd just heard. She wanted to see pictures and know what her twin was like. It was starting to make sense—the dreams, the nagging void, the feeling that there was something more, and finally, the indescribable part of her life that was always missing.

"Mom, can I see a picture of him? Do you have any?"

Alex nodded, almost relieved to be free of secrets. Amber's life had drastically changed in a matter of moments, but they could now begin to work on the healing process.

Alex went into the attic and brought two large boxes down.

She handed them to Amber, and they sat on the living room floor thumbing through each picture. Amber ran her finger over one of them where she was actually sitting next to her brother playing with a toy. They were both smiling. She held it next to her heart for a moment and let the tears fall where they may.

They carefully went through each item: Kevin's baby blanket, his shoes, his little hat, his christening outfit, and lastly, his fingerprints on the hospital release form. That was all they had left of him.

Hours passed, and it was approaching dinner time. The phone rang numerous times, but they let it go to voicemail. They were both so starved and exhausted. Their uneaten burgers had grown stale, and they decided to order a pizza. No words were shared between them. For now, just focusing on Kevin's memory was enough to fill the uncomfortable silence. After dinner, Amber grabbed Kevin's baby blanket and excused herself to go to sleep. She cuddled against it, nestling her face in it, and let dreams flow effortlessly into her head.

Chapter 37

The next morning, Zach awoke feeling more refreshed than he had in a very long time. He was overcome by the need to go for a vigorous walk and stretch his muscles. He'd slept for almost fifteen hours, his body needing to catch up after his intense nights of vicious murders.

He didn't think it would be necessary to harm anyone today. He felt energized and in a good mood. While not a big fan of coffee, he did love the taste of cola. He went outside to enjoy a large glass of it while enjoying the somewhat cooler weather that only the morning would offer.

As he stepped outside, Zach saw a blue sports car going way too fast on the small street. It turned around the corner at sixty miles per hour, nearly running over an older woman and clipping the side of Zach's car that was parked in front of his driveway. It was a common occurrence for people to drive like lunatics here, but no one had ever hit his car before.

The driver didn't even stop. It seemed too early to be drunk, but it looked like this guy'd had a bit too much fun partying the night before.

Zach walked over to his car to examine the damages and saw his bumper lying before him and a flat tire on the left passenger side. It seemed that once the flat was fixed, it would still be drivable. He looked up for any sign of this person, but not a trace was found.

He was still calm at this point, but upset about the complete disregard this person had for ruining another person's property. He put the cola in the hood of the car, opened his trunk and began to fix his flat. He threw his bumper in the trunk as well, disregarded his previous need to take a walk, and started up the engine. Putting his car in gear, he drove off with no set destination in mind.

He pulled into the gas station, and, as luck would have it, there was his new-found, reckless friend pumping gas. Zach pulled up right behind him and got out of the car.

"Drive a little fast, don't ya?" Zach asked, surveying the man's car. He saw some paint chips, but no devastating damage.

"What's it to you? What the hell do you care?" The man was approximately forty years old and well dressed in his pressed jeans and navy blue button down shirt. He was the type of person who looked down upon others and Zach was even surprised to see him pumping his own gas.

"Well, normally I wouldn't care," Zach said calmly. "Normally I wouldn't give a shit if you drove a little fast into a brick wall and turned your head into a pumpkin, but you almost ran over an elderly woman who was minding her own business, and you successfully managed to take off my entire bumper, as well as cause my tire to go flat. *That's* what it is to me."

The man gave Zach a condescending smirk and looked at the front of his car. "If you ask me, I did you a favor. That car is a piece of shit. Here's a quarter. Go buy yourself a new bumper." He threw a coin at Zach.

"I happen to like my car, and you can keep your change. Give me the money for the bumper, and I'll let it go."

"The hell with you. You want the money? Come and get it. You know who you're dealing with? I'm the president of SGS, Incorporated. You know the building. The beautiful one a person like you could never afford. Come meet me there. It'll be just you and me, pal. I gave the staff the day off, being that it is Saturday and all. Aren't I a great boss?

You can come there anytime, but your type—you don't have the guts."

The man got in his car and sped away faster than Zach could reply. He shrugged his shoulders and opened his trunk, pulled out a gas can, and filled it halfway. He then walked into the minimart and bought a pack of Camels and a lighter, even though he'd never smoked a day in his life. He couldn't stand the smell of cigarettes. As far as he was concerned, he would rather die of something more exciting than an illness brought on by years of inhaling tar-filled smoke sticks.

Zach knew exactly where SGS was. Oddly enough, he'd worked there as a janitor last summer when he was fourteen and got paid cash, off the books. He lied about his age, and they believed him. It was a beautiful office, and he remembered the building and the layout quite well. He figured he ought to go visit the president, after all.

The breeze picked up, blowing leaves and debris around as he pulled into the SGS parking lot. He parked around back, even though the only car in the front parking lot was that of his reckless driver friend.

SGS was a paper goods store that sold all types of greeting cards, fliers, brochures, business cards, banners, etc. If you could write on it, they sold it. On Saturdays, they always left the back door unlocked for deliveries.

Zach opened his trunk, took out his gas can, and opened the back door to the building. He did a quick look around. As expected, no one was roaming the halls. He dumped the gas around the perimeter of the warehouse and reached in his pocket for a cigarette.

As he lit it, he coughed and almost gagged but thought *mind over matter* as he flicked the lit cigarette to the far corner where he'd first dumped the gas. He lit another one quickly and threw it a little closer. As the flames picked up speed through the warehouse, he lit two more cigarettes at once and flicked them in separate directions.

He flung the rest of the cigarettes and the lighter into the middle of the warehouse. The paper goods ignited within seconds, and the sole commodity of SGS was ablaze. Coughing and teary eyed, Zach covered his mouth and ran out the open back door, making sure to leave it open so the wind would help feed the fire expediently.

He hopped in his car and skidded away. He hadn't been as careful as he normally was, as this was broad daylight, but he was still quite confident he wouldn't be caught.

Chapter 38

Amber woke up still clutching Kevin's blanket, mourning for a brother she once knew and loved but couldn't remember anything about. Similar to her feelings for her father, she felt that if she held onto one item that once belonged to Kevin, she would somehow feel closer to him.

She woke up feeling not quite comforted but actually a little scared. She dreamt she was going on her first job interview. In real life, she hadn't yet experienced her first job but was looking forward to it when she turned sixteen.

She walked into a beautiful building surrounded by palm trees positioned on the hill of a dead-end street. It seemed to be located in a tropical area, somewhere beautiful where the sky was bright blue and the sun blanketed the city, generating temperatures of over one hundred degrees. She looked for the elevator, found it down the first hallway, and pushed the button for up. As she stepped on, she saw a young man inside smiling a malicious grin.

He had a red gas can and was spilling gas all around them, along the walls of the elevator. She had tried to joke with him and make light of the situation in hopes that he would stop, and that the situation wasn't what she thought it to be, but all he said to her was, "If you want to live, you better leave."

As he said that, he lit a cigarette and looked her in the eyes. His eyes were black and cold, but he had a beautiful face. It was haunting. It was the same face she saw in all her dreams. He entranced her with his stare, but she knew she had to get out of the elevator to save herself. She asked him one question, "What about you, though?" As she did so, he began to flick his cigarette, and the flames grew tall.

There was no time to hear his answer or to save the lives of those who would be caught in the trailing flames. She had no idea how many people were in the building or if there was a feasible escape plan for them.

Running top speed out of the elevator, she stumbled her way through the maze of doors, tripped over a large box, and crawled her way toward the outside door.

As she reached the parking lot, she took a deep breath and gulped the fresh air as the flames encompassed the inside of the building, a big burst of orange and blue silhouettes dancing erratically. Black smoke billowed through the air as the lives of innocent people came to a screeching halt. She ran to her car, and as she turned the key, she watched the once-beautiful building blow to pieces.

Through the flames, the madman walked out as if he were invincible. He was unharmed and looked like he was running, but not because he was scared. He was headed down to another building at the bottom of the hill. She had a chance to try to save those people at least, but he was already ahead of her by a long shot. There would be no way.

Toward the side of the building, she saw an open door. She could at least warn them.

Moving as fast as she could, she opened her car door and fled to the open door, screaming as loud as she could for everyone to leave. They all just looked at her, but it was too late. Flames were engulfing the office. In order to survive, she needed to escape.

Once again, her night of sleep was interrupted by some horrific dream that held no meaning but woke her up either screaming, sweating, out of breath, scared out of her mind, or a combination of all four. She didn't stay asleep long enough to find out how the dream ended.

Was she really going crazy? Experts and psychoanalysts will sometimes say that a person can't handle past traumatic experiences, so the mind finds a way to deal with it while they are asleep, sort of like a safety mechanism.

She knew her past—all of it now. There were no secrets. From what she understood, she was never harmed and never put in harm's way.

Sure, losing a father and a brother at such a young age was a traumatic experience, but to have continued dreams like this? There had to be something wrong with her.

Chapter 39

As Zach pulled around the corner, he swore that he was in the clear, safe and unnoticed. Quite pleased with himself, he took one last look at the man's car in the parking lot while watching the flames destroy what was left of the building. He was certain Mr. President was no longer a man of flesh and bones. He should be ashes in mere seconds.

He continued driving, keeping watch in his rearview mirror. No flashing lights; no cops.

He parked in front of his small apartment and turned off the engine, walked up to his front door, and walked right in. As he shut the door behind him, he took a final look to scout out the neighborhood.

No cops in sight. He'd pulled it off without a hitch. His heart was racing. This was an unconventional, unplanned kill that just happened. He had woken up in a relaxed state, and the rest of the chips just fell into place. This guy clearly deserved to be killed. Three in three days.

What Zach didn't realize was that the case against him was already building. The men from the "caveyard graveyard," as Zach liked to call it, happened to have called the cops yesterday. They didn't trust Zach's story and asked the police to check it out.

The police searched the area with cadaver dogs and stumbled upon evidence of over ten dead bodies, all, of course, reduced to just bones scattered about. The men also gave a description of Zach's car. They took the license plate number too, but Zach had already disposed of that.

On the other side of town, a witness had caught a glimpse of Zach's car as he was pulling into SGS's parking lot. He also saw him leave and noted the direction he was driving.

By noon the following day, the police had run checks on makes and models of cars fitting that description. Zach didn't even have a license, so he sure as hell didn't have the car registered.

They put an alert on television for anyone who knew of a car of that model to please just let the cops know so they could check it out. Most of the leads were legit; the cars were registered to decent folks earning a decent living who hadn't so much as a parking ticket on their records.

Their third to last lead was the one that let them to their possible suspect. A concerned neighbor gave the police station a call while staring at the car positioned right in front of the driveway next door.

At noon, Zach awoke to, "POLICE! OPEN UP!"

He thought he was dreaming. As he became fully awake, the quick realization set in that he was cornered. There was only the back entrance, which was probably swarming with police; no windows from which to escape. He didn't own an actual gun, and a knife or a hammer wouldn't overpower an officer with a gun.

This was how it was going to end. He couldn't remember if he'd locked his door or not, since he typically didn't worry about that type of thing.

Surprisingly, he wasn't upset. He didn't value his own life too much. He didn't want to go to jail but figured he could talk his way out of this one. An accident, perhaps? With any luck, he'd just get put away for arson. Maybe Mr. President didn't die in the fire. But even though the risk of imprisonment was there, he secretly hoped that he had. The only way he could know is if he opened the door.

Before he approached reality, he reached into his hidden safe and took all of the money he had with him, just in case. It totaled one thousand dollars. It wasn't a lot of money, but he had gotten by on a lot less. That usually lasted him about three months, including rent. If he had to live in a cave, it would last him a lot longer. He turned the knob and opened the door. "Hello, officer."

"Hands where I can see 'em. Is that your car?"

"Yes, it is," Zach said in the calmest of tones.

"We got a report that you were at the scene of a crime over the past few days. Were you anywhere near SGS?"

"I might've been. I know I drove past it."

"What's your name, sir?"

"My name is Zach."

"Zach, do you have a last name?"

He didn't. "Jacobs."

"Zach Jacobs, huh? Have any ID?"

Zach shook his head no, and the cop started reading him his Miranda rights as he prepared to handcuff him. "You have the right to remain silent. Anything you say can and will be used against you in a court of law…"

Zach was very respectful and turned on his charm full force. He didn't admit to anything other than being near the scene of the crime. The worst thing was that he hadn't had time to wash the gasoline smell out of his car, though he remembered being extremely careful not to spill any of it. He would just have to hope for the best at this point.

The news media swarmed all over this fire. Apparently Mr. SGS President was an important man. He hadn't made it out of the building in time. Zach was pleased with himself about that. *Turned that smug son of a bitch's smile upside down.*

This was the first time he had killed anyone during the day and didn't have to drag their body into the secluded desert. He'd apologize to the coyotes later for not giving them a meal.

Just as the policeman attempted to slap on the cuffs, a car came spinning around the corner, way too fast again, only this time causing a head-on collision with another car.

As the cop turned to look, Zach took the opportunity to break into a run. At this point in time, being fifteen was a full advantage. He was strong and used to walking long distances with at least a two-hundred-pound corpse on his shoulders, so he was able to run top speed without even getting winded.

The cops on the scene started to run after him on foot; some got in their cop cars, but the accident that had just occurred blocked the street. There was no way they could chase him by car. The leading police officer went to take a shot at Zach, but way too many civilians milled around outside after hearing the car crash. If he took a shot, an innocent bystander was sure to get hurt.

Zach was gone. He was usually able to outrun anyone, and he could hotwire a car in less than thirty seconds.

He ran into an older part of town about two miles away from his house and quickly got to work. Most of the people in the house whose car he was hotwiring were either too drunk or drugged up to realize someone was outside messing with their belongings. By the time they did realize it, Zach would be long gone. He just hoped the car had enough gas and would actually run.

As luck would have it, the car not only had a full tank, but someone had left twenty dollars sitting on the console. At this point, every little bit helped.

He tried to drive away as calmly as possible and then, once clear, took off like a bandit. He was sure there would be road blocks soon, but if he was fast enough, he would just miss them.

Chapter 40

The police sent out search teams looking for their suspect, who, by now, they were convinced was guilty.

They ransacked his tiny apartment for any clues of who this Zach Jacobs person really was and what he was all about. They searched for souvenirs from his victims but couldn't find anything. Most serial killers kept souvenirs as a little sickly reminder of all of the "work" they had done. It was something to keep them proud.

The only thing they found in this apartment were a few unopened bottles of alcohol; an old couch; some older clothes; some library books, none of which were overdue; a minimal supply of food in the refrigerator; and a live tarantula. This type of killer was unprecedented. The more unique the profile of the killer, the harder it would be to find him.

Though the apartment left much to be desired, Zach was no slob. Everything was in its proper place, and nothing seemed carelessly thrown around.

Investigators were lucky to find his ID on the table. Even though it was fake, it did have his picture on it. That was a big help to them, because other than that, there were no pictures of Zach Jacobs anywhere to be found, and they doubted that he had ever had another picture taken.

They would be able to show this picture on the evening news and send out an alert for everyone to keep their eyes peeled for someone looking like him. He was to be considered armed and dangerous. They wondered where all of his weapons were that he'd used to gruesomely kill his victims; they found none in the house.

They searched the car as well, and, other than a few small knives hardly capable of killing someone, they found nothing. They would search the car for hair, fibers, blood, anything that could be used as evidence—and they were confident they would find some.

That would be one of the best case scenarios; however, the better case would be if they could track down Zach.

He couldn't run forever, and they doubted that someone like him had many friends, although some serial killers had charming, likable personalities that caused people to trust them implicitly.

From the few seconds the one cop spent speaking to Zach, he was afraid that this was the case. He felt confident that some poor soul was going to have a chance meeting with him and give him access to whatever he needed. Zach would probably return the favor by bludgeoning the person to death, although they couldn't say for sure what triggered him to kill.

It could be for no reason at all, or he could have actually known his victims. They didn't believe the latter was correct. For the amount of bones found, they figured they had about ten bodies. There could be more farther out into the desert or in another location altogether.

The search teams were working around the clock to try and gather clues. They figured he just killed when he felt like it, with no rhyme or reason. They wouldn't know for sure until they caught him.

Chances were he would stay in hiding for a while, but judging by the number of times he had done it, the need to kill would be too great. They just hoped they would find him before he gathered any more victims. That was their first priority.

It was kind of like a catch-22. In order to catch him, he would have to come out of hiding. In order for him to come out of hiding, he would most likely be about to kill.

By the looks of it, this person was no more than sixteen, seventeen years old at the most. The smarts and know-how he displayed at this age could only mean imminent danger going forward.

Time was of the essence at this stage of the game, and they needed to find him quickly.

Chapter 41

Tiffany and Amber hadn't spoken since their night at the bowling alley. It was unusual for them, but Tiffany just figured Amber was busy with all of the plans they had discussed and decided to stay in and just watch television. Curiosity was killing her, but she wanted to give her friend a little more time.

As she did just that, the first thing she noticed was a special news report about a company in Las Vegas. Apparently, this company had been set on fire and one person had died. They flashed a picture of the CEO on the screen—the thirty-eight year old, self-proclaimed millionaire of a paper goods store. Tiffany added "good-looking" to his bio and said out loud, though no one was listening, "Such a shame."

They then showed the suspect and said that he had escaped. Tiffany couldn't believe what she was looking at. She picked up the phone and immediately called her best friend.

"Amber, turn on Channel 2 News. You have to see this."

Amber was still not in the mood to be social, not even with Tiffany."

"Stop being stubborn; just do it! This could be your twin brother—he looks just like you."

Amber froze. Tiffany had no idea of the conversation that took place with Jill at her father's job or the conversation that Amber and her mother had had. Those last five words she had just said to her friend hit Amber harder than she could imagine.

Amber was in the living room with her mother and gave in to her friend. "OK, Tiffany," she sighed. She wanted to scream at her but knew her friend was just trying to be funny.

She turned on the television and switched it to channel two. When the picture came to the screen, Amber grew somber and looked at her mom. "Tiffany, I have to go." Not only did he look like Amber, but it could have easily been the same boy from her dreams.

"Wait! Doesn't he look just like you? I mean, put some long hair on him and he is your twin. What a wacko! He just set this place on fire. They think he might be linked to some other murders. They found bones of victims hidden in the desert. This is sick shit! He is one freaking psychopath!"

"*Tiffany*. I have to go!"

Amber slammed the phone down and looked at her mom. "Mom, is it possible? He looks just like me, maybe a bit older, but look at the features on him. You can't deny it's like looking right at me!" Amber's eyes were tearful.

Alex just sat staring. She thought she would know those eyes anywhere. They mesmerized her when he was a year old, and they were the same beautiful features, except without the genuine innocence and gentleness they used to possess.

She would bet her life that this person on the news, the one they were calling Zach, was really her son. That was really Kevin. She wanted to appear calm and collected in Amber's eyes. "Honey, let's just watch a little more. He does look like you, but sweetheart, Kevin was an angel. He passed away a long time ago."

She thought that if she had ever heard news of her son being found alive, she would feel elated as she was be able to salvage at least one piece of her life that was missing. But if this was indeed her son, she had feelings of despair almost worse than when she found out he was kidnapped, mixed with a glimmer of hope that she could see him again, talk to him, tell him he was loved his whole life.

As the story unraveled, it seems this boy had set that building on fire. A day prior, two men from the Las Vegas County Department had come in contact with someone looking very similar to him and very suspicious. He was parked in a secluded area with what seemed like blood stains surrounding his car. The men called the police, who then walked into the desert and stumbled across some bones. They thought it was just wildlife, but the forensic specialist identified it as human remains.

They described the man and the car he owned to the police. He was almost arrested but escaped when a freak accident took place in the exact location of the arrest.

As the police searched the area some more, they came across dozens upon dozens more human remains, all piled on top of each other near a small cave. Some were scattered around nearby.

Alex stared at the cold-faced killer on the screen of her television and her mind flashed back to fourteen years ago as she stared into the trusting eyes of her one-year-old boy. She'd let him down. She thought of the place where Steve's dead body was found and started to shudder. He was found in Las Vegas as well. This had to be Kevin. "Amber, we're going to Las Vegas. I don't know if it's Kevin, but I'll never forgive myself if I don't find out for sure."

"Mom, is it possible? A killer? And a *serial* killer at that?"

"Amber, I never thought it possible for Kevin to be alive, so although this sounds weird, don't get your hopes up. Everyone supposedly has a "double"—someone who looks like them. I'm sure that's what this is.

"I have to admit, though, Steve's body was found not far from where this young man lives. If it's him, it has to be a mistake. He could never be violent. He was just too much of a sweetheart. He was loved by both your father and me. He was also adored by you, even though you don't remember. People who are raised like that don't become killers."

"But Mom," Amber carefully interjected, "he wasn't *raised* by you. I'm sorry to say this so bluntly, but it could be him, and he could be guilty. We have to think of the what-ifs." Amber sometimes sounded more like the adult. She was very mature for her age and was able to introduce logic before emotion in *some* situations. For now, she was able to remain logical.

Alex went online and started looking into flights for Las Vegas. She'd never been and had certainly never dreamed that this would be the reason she would be going. She was terrified. If this was her son, he would be taken from her again, either hauled off to jail or sentenced to death. They hadn't caught him yet, but she was confident they would—and she wanted to be there.

Would she rather that her baby be dead as she thought him to be all of these years, or did she want to know this cold-hearted killer was actually her son?

She booked their flight for first thing in the morning and checked in online. She also found a hotel away from The Strip. She didn't think they would quite be in the mood for glitz and glamour under the circumstances. "Amber, can you miss school for a few days? You'd be out for about five of them."

"Yeah. I only have one absence, and that was yesterday."

"Good. Please get me the number for the school so I can leave a message, and then go pack your things. One way or another, we need to find out about this person they are claiming to be responsible for all of those horrendous killings. I don't think either of us will ever be able to sleep again if there's any doubt whether or not he may or may not be my son and your brother. We're going to Vegas."

Chapter 42

They woke up early in preparation for their flight and drove to the airport in silence, but not before Alex took Kevin's baby fingerprints, as well as a picture from the newspaper of Steve Johnson. She wanted to show it to the person they called 'Zach' to see if he knew Steve, thus proving he was her son. If she ever got the chance to do so.

There was no turbulence on the flight, which was helpful since they were both nursing a sick, twisted feeling in the pits of their stomachs. They were served a tiny banana muffin and coffee or soda, along with some chips later on.

They arrived in Vegas at two o'clock in the afternoon. They waited on the cab line at the airport, hailed a cab, and went downtown to the police station to try and find out any information they could. They wanted to make sure they went through the proper channels.

Both Alex and Amber felt nauseated. The closer they got to the station, the more they wanted to turn around and go home. Alex had been waiting fourteen years to find out *anything at all* on the whereabouts and the fate of her young child. She never got any closure, and this void had a huge impact on her life.

Amber only found out the truth a few days ago, and just in time too, only to find out her *twin* may be alive and well, and possibly convicted of murdering at least ten people.

Once they arrived at the station, they asked the driver to wait around until they got out, promising him full payment. He agreed and waited in the parking lot.

It had been a long day already, flying from New York to Las Vegas, and both mother and daughter just wanted to go to sleep, but they had to find out the truth. They wouldn't sleep until they did, and even then it would be difficult.

As they approached the stairs to the station, Amber had a flashback to her dreams and had to sit down. She actually stopped breathing for a moment and clutched at her throat, grasping for air.

"Amber, what's wrong?!"

She looked at her mother and just said, "I know that Kevin is this person they are calling Zach. I'm sorry, Mom." Her dreams were all about him. She saw the horrific things he did while she was sleeping. He shared the vision with her somehow, either knowingly or unknowingly. It was the twin bond people spoke of.

It was clearer to her now than it ever had been, and she just repeated herself to her mother. "It's him. Let's go inside." Now more than ever, she wanted to find out the truth. She wasn't sure whether she should be excited or terrified.

Alex brought Kevin's fingerprints to the front desk and explained her story. The woman there told Alex they could put these against Zach's fingerprints that they had dusted from inside his apartment and determine if they were a match. It might take a few days, however.

She them to a fifteen-by-fifteen waiting room with a small metal table in the middle. The metal folding chairs around it looked like they were going to collapse the moment they sat on them. The adjoining door to the hallway had one small window, and that was it. The grey walls contributed to the somber, utterly depressing ambiance.

An officer walked in, and they both looked up. Alex spoke with him with tears in her eyes and began to ask some relevant questions. No one really knew much at this point, but she was hoping to gain some type of knowledge and see what she could do to help.

"Can you please tell me about Kevin, the boy that is being accused of these horrific crimes?"

"Ma'am, his name is Zach. Are you looking for someone else?"

"I'm sorry. Zach. I think I may be able to help find him."

"I'm all ears." His sarcastic inflection wasn't lost on Alex; however, she wanted her story to be heard.

Alex began discussing the events that had possibly shaped Kevin into the person he was today. "Fourteen years ago, there was a murder." The guard's eyes drifted from Alex to Amber as he wondered where this story was going in a town filled with crazy people.

"My husband was the one murdered, by a man named Steve Johnson. I believe his body was found five years ago in a run-down apartment building. This man, Steve, attempted to kill me and almost succeeded. He managed to render me unconscious for two days, and as he did, he kidnapped my one-year-old son, Kevin. Kevin is Amber's brother," Alex said, pointing to Amber. "Her twin brother.

"I'm quite certain Steve never told Kevin— or as you call him, *Zach*— the truth. Kevin may never have known he had a mother and a sister who would be there for him. As far as he is concerned, he may think he is all alone."

The officer looked down at them and yawned, as if he were bored with their story and couldn't wait for them to leave.

Alex regarded his blank stare with a much more firm and strict voice this time. "Look, I'm not one of your typical, crazy fanatics who collect serial killer paraphernalia. This isn't a story I conjured up to get on the evening news. Believe me, I'd give anything in this world to have back the life I had fourteen years ago—a loving husband and a toddler who adored and trusted me. Those days are long gone.

"So if you're going to sit here and stare at me condescendingly, find me someone who is capable of doing their job, and someone who has the best interests of everyone involved in the case, including the innocent people of Las Vegas, at heart. If my son is as dangerous as you claim him to be, then you're solely responsible for wasting precious time."

She paused for his reaction and then continued. "Are you ready to listen to me instead of counting the minutes until your next meal?"

He stared at her for a moment, suddenly realizing she was from the East Coast and had brought that aggressive, take-no-shit personality with her.

"Ma'am, please continue."

She took a deep breath. "So, as I see it, it may be beneficial to have us on the news, in case he is watching. I realize it's a long shot, but it may be one worth taking. You can't deny the exact similarities between my daughter's face and this person you call Zach. If he sees her, he won't be able to deny it either. If nothing else, curiosity may bring him closer. Then we can all get closure."

She had a point. The officer had nothing to lose, and if this brought him in, he had everything to gain. He had been longing for a big break in order to get the prestige he felt he so well deserved—and the pay raise that went along with it.

"Wait here." The cop went to get his superior to see if putting these two ladies on the news was a possibility.

Within minutes, they had the news team on the phone with an offer for a breaking story.

As he returned to the make-shift waiting room, his whole demeanor had changed and his previous nonchalant attitude now leaned more toward anxious and caring.

"Ladies, I spoke to the powers that be, and they liked your idea to go on the evening news. We thank you for your courage to do this. Is there anything I can get for you: coffee, soda, cookies perhaps?

"We're fine," Alex said. "Just let us know when we can tell our story." The truth was that they were starving but were so nervous that they wanted to get this over with as soon as possible. Amber walked out to pay and dismiss the cabbie, as it might be hours before they left the station.

At around 4:30 p.m., the Channel 3 News team showed up with their cameras ready. They were promised an exclusive at the moment, so no competition would be invited. They could, however, be waiting outside of the station once the interview session was over.

At 5:00 p.m., they were ready to go live. Shane Matten was the reporter interviewing them, and he was as professional as they get. Alex was happy that at least one person she'd met here had some sense. Everyone else seemed to have a hidden agenda or a nonchalant attitude, showing they only cared about themselves and nothing else.

For her to find out the truth she needed to trust at least one person who was capable, and Shane seemed to fit that role.

"Live from Channel 3, we have a message for Zach Jacobs, one you may find very interesting, so please listen up and pay close attention. Your mother and sister have come forward to speak to you."

They told the entire story from start to finish about how they were related and what had happened many years prior.

They could only hope that wherever Zach was, he had access to a television, newspaper, or radio. Hopefully he was egotistical and would wonder what was being said about him. Otherwise, this was all for nothing.

Chapter 43

Zach had no access to television; it wasn't like he could just pick one up and plug it into a tree. He was curious, however, and wanted to know just what the cops knew about him, whether they had his fingerprints, his weapons, or other incriminating evidence.

He was certain he'd left his one ID behind, and he kicked himself for doing so. Now they have a picture of him to flash around town and use in their search. That was sloppy of him.

Thankfully, the car he stole had gas in it, and he made it past the state line into Utah. He chose to travel east, as there were many more states to choose from. For now, he camped out in what seemed like a desolate area.

He parked the car in an exceptionally bad neighborhood, in hopes that it would be stolen. He then walked a few miles, stole another car, and drove a little more. He picked up a few items from a 7-Eleven being run by a careless, drug addict teenager who barely looked up when Zach cashed out. The punk cashier was too busy flirting with one of the other workers, who looked as useless as he did.

One of the items Zach did pick up was a newspaper, special edition. Unfortunately for him, there was a small blurb on the front cover. The 7-Eleven junkies didn't even notice. Amazing how a baseball cap and sunglasses can alter one's appearance.

He couldn't wait to get to his final destination to see just what was being said about him and how misinformed the media must be.

He pulled off in a desolate area and scouted out how far the walk would be to a nearby but secluded place to set up camp. He figured a two-mile walk would suffice. He parked the car and gathered his things.

Before he began his journey, he opened up the newspaper and was genuinely surprised by what he read. The story told of how he'd escaped being caught by the police officers by something as ironic as a car accident taking place right there, blocking off the entire road. Zach laughed, as he couldn't have planned that better himself.

This was going to be good. Two ladies claiming to be his relatives. That was fantastic. Like that was possible. What would they think of next? Where have you been the last fifteen years, or however old I am? "I hope they have pictures," he said to himself as he started his walk, looking forward to a good read.

Once he settled down in a remote area under a bunch of trees, he began reading with a flashlight he'd picked up at the store. He covered himself in some authentic southwestern blankets he'd picked up, got cozy, ate some premium beef jerky, and read the story.

He chuckled to himself, shaking his head at the ridiculous lengths some people would go to just to be in the media—and then he turned the page.

He wasn't chuckling anymore. Two photographs on the page in front of him made him try to focus in just a bit more, borrowing light from the moon and stars, along with his flashlight. Though the flashlight produced plenty of light for him to see clearly by, he was mesmerized by the image laid out on the black and white pages in front of him.

There was no mistaking it. Either someone out there was truly his double, or these women were telling the truth. What scared him was that the girl slightly resembled the girl from one of his dreams, and though he didn't get freaked out easily, he was feeling a bit uneasy.

It could just be wishful thinking, but Zach had always felt that this wasn't the life he was supposed to have. He felt there was something bigger and better out there that was meant to be for him. He cursed under his breath, and a blind rage built up inside of him. If this was true, he was the product of a happy and loving marriage, and Joe was this Steve person they spoke about.

As he turned the next page, his theory was proven true. There was a picture of the very person whom Zach had called Joe for the first ten years of his life. This person who was solely responsible for molding him into the monster he was today. This was the same lowlife excuse for a man who had cowardly murdered Zach's own father fourteen years before and stolen his very life from him.

Anger and frustration burned through his veins. Although he had helped push Joe/Steve, down the stairs, it wasn't enough. He wanted to go back in time and torture him over and over again. He wanted to be one hundred percent responsible for his death. As ridiculous as he knew it was, he couldn't help but feel that way. There was nothing he could do about it; the man was already dead, but that didn't help matters.

He held back a scream that had been lingering for the past fifteen years. It was one that would have a boisterous roar in the beginning and virtually no end. Tears of intense rage built up, scorching his eyes. He had no place to release his anger, nowhere to run, and he couldn't nestle in the confines of the tiny, pathetic apartment he called home. Compared to living outdoors, that home was a palace.

The only comfort he found was in the intense darkness available in the tiny alcove that, for tonight, doubled as his sleeping quarters. It was the only thing that seemed to mirror the image of his tortured soul.

This was the first time in his life that he had ever experienced such a severe range of emotions. He has been angry before and had had some bouts of a minor depression, usually cured by a good kill. He had never before felt so misguided, so confused, so full of hatred, and even a little regret.

Dangling in front of him like a small carrot was the family he had longed for his entire life. They were probably the type who lounged around the living room next to a warm fire at Christmas time, singing carols and exchanging presents.

After seeing the pictures, he had no doubt this was the way he was supposed to be raised, and he knew that he could never meet them. Once he came out of hiding, he would be put in jail. He was fairly confident this was the case. Although that thought didn't scare him too badly, since he was still considered a juvenile, it would take away his freedom and his ability to kill whenever the need presented itself.

No, he had to keep moving. He lit a fire and threw the newspaper into it, watching shades of orange with a blue tip flicker in the inferno, spreading pieces of ash throughout the open space.

Then he did something he'd never in his life been known to do—he cried himself to sleep. He sobbed until he couldn't breathe and let his eyes close on their own as he lay next to the fire.

As he slept, he dreamt of the life he should've had. He envisioned the father who had once rocked him to sleep and felt the gentle hands of his loving mother, whose soft features looked so gentle, loving, and harmless.

Next to him was his sister, who quietly played while he watched protectively. It was the most peaceful feeling he'd had in a long while and the most relaxed he had ever been.

If only it were real.

Chapter 44

Alex and Amber had no choice but to leave the station once the news broadcast had ended. Now it was just a question of waiting and seeing. They called a cab and waited patiently for it to arrive.

They asked him to take them to their hotel, Bella Luna, right off of The Strip. No words needed to be said. Right now, silence was the exact comfort that they needed. The cab driver, unfortunately, didn't feel the same way. He possessed the rugged, crass attitude one might expect while watching an unrealistic film, yet here he was, driving them around.

"So, visiting your boyfriend today? Both of you have relations with some of the jailbirds-to-be? That's OK. Everyone needs loving, don't they?" He was more concerned with talking to them than focusing on the road.

"Please just take us to our hotel," Alex said, exhausted. "Who we know is really none of your damn business."

"Oh, *sorry*. Just making conversation. I didn't know you were going to get an attitude about it. You're in Vegas, lady. Lighten up. I'm sure your daughter here is looking to have some fun here. She is your daughter, right? Oh, no. Is she your girlfriend? Whoa. Am I getting it all wrong?"

No comment came from the backseat. Alex's eyes were burning, not only from crying but from wanting to tear the eyes out of this driver's skull.

Influxes of emotion streamed through her mind. For the past fourteen years, she'd prayed every night that her son was alive somewhere, healthy and somehow unharmed. One could argue that her prayers had been answered. He was alive, and he seemed healthy from the way he had outrun the cops. Physically, he didn't look harmed in his picture.

It was the life he had been given that had caused him to transform into the monster that he was. Though it was yet to be proven in a court of law, she had looked into his eyes in his photograph and seen that they were empty. The lovely innocence that she saw when she looked into his eyes that awful night so many years ago was all gone. All she saw now was hurt, hatred, and darkness.

Other than giving him money for a lawyer and maybe buying him a suit and possibly a meal, there was nothing she or anyone could do for him. If convicted, he would certainly be facing the death penalty. His only saving grace was that he was still under the age of eighteen, but Alex could already tell he didn't want to be saved.

He was deprived of a life that should've been his. It should've been filled with love, family, and happiness. Instead it was filled with what must have been abuse and misery. She didn't know any of it and doubted he would ever tell her. Why should he?

Amber was manifesting dark thoughts of her own. She had just looked at a photograph into the eyes of a brother, a twin brother, that until a few days ago she didn't know that she had. She had a flashback to her dreams and noted that he was the same boy who kept reappearing in them.

How was it that she was to be the lucky one? She was the only one unharmed by the events that took place that evening. If Kevin wasn't cranky that night, he would've been lying in the crib next to Amber's, safe and sound. Her father's killer most likely would've just run off. What if it had been Amber who was on the front porch? Would Steve have kidnapped her? Would it have mattered that she was a girl?

She wondered just what exactly possessed Kevin to kill those innocent people. Was the abuse he suffered so terrible that there was just nothing left inside, no heart and no soul? How could someone who looked like her and was once inseparable from her be so heartless?

She cried for her brother, her mother, and her father. She sobbed for the families whose lives were stolen by her brother. Though he was guilty, his upbringing was due to no fault of his own. He couldn't have helped it, could he? She might never know.

She leaned toward her mother and, like on the car ride home from the hospital fourteen years ago, Alex buried her face in Amber's hair and let tears fall from her eyes.

They finally arrived at the hotel. Thankfully the taxi driver had stopped talking gibberish minutes earlier. They gave him his fare along with a minimal tip and brought their belongings into the hotel.

It wasn't fancy, but it was beautiful and clean. Had they been here under different circumstances, they would've enjoyed the stunning view from the room. They were on the south side off of The Strip but were able to catch the bright lights from a far enough distance.

Past the flashy hotels and glowing signs, the landscape was surrounded by multi-colored mountains, ranging from vibrant reds to earthy sand colors, still capped with snow from the winter flurries. The valley, of course, did not have any snow but was saturated with bright sunshine from the blue, cloudless sky above.

The room had two double beds, and on the walls hung beautiful paintings of a seemingly tranquil setting. Most people came to Las Vegas to enjoy the exciting nightlife, get drunk, do drugs, and go to a neighboring town where prostitution was *not* illegal. To go there looking for a serial killer son who had been abducted at the tender age of one wasn't the norm.

They were both exhausted, given the events of the past two days. They knew they should speak and get it out, but somehow, the quiet was more serene. Talking would only confirm the reality that they didn't have the heart to face.

"Mom, are you alright?"

Alex shook her head and let her eyes drift down the wall to an outlet that had been slightly painted over. Her eyes then wandered to the ceiling as if by searching the room, she could find the right answers and would know what to do and say. If only it were that easy.

She finally looked at her daughter and took a deep breath. She attempted an apologetic smile but couldn't force her mouth to make even the slightest sign of a happy face.

"Amber, I can't find the right words to describe my emotions. Where do I begin? First off, I want to rule out self-pity, but it is so abundantly there.

"After that, there's such regret. Regret that I took Kevin onto the porch that night. Regret that months prior, I'd run into Steve at your father's job and didn't say anything then about how nervous and uneasy he made me feel. Regret that I couldn't save my son when a raged psycho killer came to my home and abducted him.

"There's elation that I might get to see my son, my first born, and tell him that I love him. Then fear that he won't believe me.

"Finally, there's despair. I know in my heart, and you might as well know, that the chances for Kevin's survival are slim. Even if he doesn't get capital punishment, he will spend his life in prison as a hardened criminal.

"You need to grasp that, Amber. I'd love to believe that he was set up and that he didn't commit those horrible crimes, but the truth is that I think he did. Though I hate to admit it, the Kevin we both knew and loved years ago…has died. What's left is a shell of his body and the torture that it had to endure."

Amber nodded her head in understanding and grabbed her mom's hand. "I can't fully comprehend what you're going through. I'm feeling only a portion of that, so I can only imagine it's multiplied for you, Mom. I have to admit, though, I'm tired. I think I need to close my eyes and take a nap."

"Good idea, Amber. When we wake up, maybe we can think more clearly. Close your eyes. We'll get a late dinner. I think we deserve to relax a little and maybe even eat something. I'll wake you in a few hours."

Chapter 45

Zach woke up nestled in his blankets, his left side of his face blazing hot from being so close to the open flame. He looked up at the sky and out to the sun rising in the east and vaguely remembered his dream.

As he became more aware, he brushed off the dream like it was burning his skin. It was one he didn't ask for and certainly didn't want. That lifestyle could never be, and he swore to himself that he wouldn't have any more unwanted dreams; not now, not ever.

He sat up and let the sun hit his face, listening to the last few softening crackles as the fire died down. Uninvited thoughts entered his mind and began to take over without his control.

Never in his life had Zach let dim-witted feelings enter his mind. He had always been level-headed, logical, and emotionless. How was it possible that two complete strangers had entered his life at a time when he needed to be on the run, only to stake their claim in his family tree?

He knew he needed to let it go, find a new stolen vehicle and go as far away as possible, move to a new state, change his appearance, and lay low for a while. In the corner of his mind, he knew all of this, so what was his obsession with doing the opposite of what the logical side of his brain was suggesting?

He had heard the good old saying that curiosity killed the cat, and he'd always strongly believed that anyone who succumbed to that type of weakness got what they deserved. Was it at all possible that he was even thinking of giving in? Was a lifetime in prison, or possibly losing his life altogether, worth finding out if these women were in fact his true birth mother and twin sister as they so defiantly claimed?

He packed up his belongings and headed toward town before the sun fully rose. He knew the police department had already set out a search party and would be looking all through Las Vegas, and most likely the neighboring cities and states as well. The sooner he found a car to steal, the better. He would have to keep switching cars. Once someone reported one stolen, the police would have a trail and a set direction in which Zach was headed.

He had planned to find a car and keep heading east, maybe travel up north a while, then back south, just to keep it interesting. He knew geography exceptionally well and was mapped out the directions in his head while jogging to find his "new" car.

He found the perfect vehicle—a small, tan sedan. It looked to be maybe five years old, and when he got inside, he discovered it had approximately eight thousand miles on it. It probably belonged to an old lady who drove it to the market and then to church and back again on Sunday mornings. Perfect. Today was Wednesday. He figured he had three full days before she would even notice it was missing.

It started right up, and no one even peeked outside the front windows. He was in luck. A song Zach recognized was playing on the radio. It wasn't necessarily a good song, something about leaving Georgia; he could relate. He substituted "Georgia" with "Utah" and began to sing along.

He started heading eastbound, looking for someplace to get a quick breakfast. After last night, he found that he was starving and needed to get something that would hold him over. The car had a half tank of gas in it, and he figured he better fill that up, as well. He had plans of driving at least fourteen hours today and wanted to be prepared, with as few interruptions as possible.

He was fortunate as there was a gas station / fast food place about a half mile down the road. That would definitely suffice. He pulled next to the first gas pump and made it a point not to meet eyes with anyone who might approach. Fortunately, no one was even out this early.

Once he finished pumping his gas, he walked into the restaurant, pretending to be digging in his pockets while ordering his meal from the cashier. An older man rang him up, a little wiser looking than the last person he ran into at 7-Eleven, but nonetheless, he didn't seem to pay attention or take any notice that he was ringing up a fugitive.

Sooner or later, Zach's luck would run out. He was going to have to work on changing his appearance altogether. He'd had plenty of time to ponder what his new look would be, but he was indecisive. He had narrowed it down to either an old hillbilly looking man or some type of woman. He'd ponder this during his drive.

Zach got in his car and noted which way was east. He positioned his breakfast in a way so that it was easily accessible while he was driving. His soda fit perfectly in the cup holder.

When no one was looking, Zach hotwired the car again and began his journey toward his new life. Unfortunately, that new life wasn't the one he had planned just fifteen minutes earlier.

Chapter 46

Alex and Amber woke up from their long-needed nap, except it was early the next morning. They'd slept straight through the night. Both felt a little refreshed but starved, so they decided to go to the restaurant downstairs, not far from the lobby. As Alex got ready, Amber thumbed through the newspaper that was left at their hotel door.

Of course, on the front page in big, bold letters, it said, "CAPTURED but GONE." Underneath was Kevin/Zach's picture. The story told of a woman who went missing last week and of the president of a company who died in a fire set by Zach.

The article described the graveyard where all of the bodies had been disposed. Amber shuddered as she read this. Could someone related to her do this? She then thought back to her dreams and froze in horror at the similarities.

Just then, her mom came out of the bathroom. "Ready, honey? Let's go get some breakfast."

They both tried to keep an upbeat attitude and didn't really care what was on the menu, as they just wanted something to fill them up. Since they'd had some sleep, a little food would help them now make an honest attempt at thinking more clearly.

After ordering and waiting for their food, they put together their next plan of attack.

"Mom, I'm certain of it. I know Kevin did all of those killings. I have no doubt." She looked down and prepared to tell her mom about the dreams she had been having over the past few years.

"Mom, remember when you walked in that morning after I had been screaming in my sleep? I was having a nightmare. One of many, actually. I hadn't told you about them, because they were all so bizarre. Some about Dad, but mostly about horrible things.

"I've only told Tiffany, and she's convinced that counseling might do me some good; however, after what I've learned over the past few days, I think I might understand now more than ever."

Her mom just stared at her intently, allowing her to go on.

"These nightmares were scary. Worse than any horror film I ever made you sit through. I think they're somehow related to Kevin.

"I read the newspaper article about him. It's pretty grim. They haven't got all of the details yet, but a woman in the neighborhood where Kevin lives went missing about a week ago. They think one of the partially decomposed bodies is hers. Some of the bodies are completely reduced to bone, as they had probably been sitting in the desert for over a year.

"One of my dreams is hauntingly similar to this graveyard they describe. So much so that I almost want to go there and see it."

Amber stopped her mother dead in her tracks before she could even open her mouth to speak. "Don't worry, I know we can't go. But, my dream was as gruesome as they are making this sound." She described her dream to her mother about the bodies in the snow/sand bank.

"I feel terrible for him and for those lives that he has single-handedly ruined," Amber said. "I wish I could say that I believe he's innocent, but those dreams! They're just too real, too related. There's no other logical explanation for them. I don't believe they're just random nightmares. I feel a connection to Kevin, only now I know exactly what it is. All of these years, I had no clue."

"Sometimes, you can see the world clearer with your eyes closed," Alex recited, as if she were recalling lines from a play.

"I've heard you say that before, Mom. What does that mean?"

"I read it as a quote once a long time ago and never understood its meaning, but now it all makes perfect sense. Those dreams were revealing the hidden truth to you, but it was so horrific, it only came to you while you were sleeping—hence when your eyes were closed. Sometimes, you can see the world clearer with your eyes closed," she repeated one last time.

"Amber, I wish that you would've told. I never want you to feel like you can't talk to me, but I do know what you mean.

"I looked at his picture and was hoping to see some sort of light in his eyes, something to show that he was my son in more than just a blood relation. I was looking for something—anything—to show that he was human, even if it were deep down beyond the years of horror that he must have endured.

"I was hoping that even though Steve abducted him, maybe, there was some chance that he treated him decent. When he first approached your father and me that night, I recall him stating how he and Garrett had wanted to adopt. All of these years, I sort of hoped that he had intentions of at least treating a child OK.

"But after looking at Kevin in his picture and seeing what I saw, I realized none of those things were true. I recognized those eyes, but his soul was missing. I wish we could help, and I think we should try, but we need to be honest with ourselves from the start. For one, if he is caught, he may not want our help. He may not admit he's related.

"Second, there might not be much we can do. Let's give it our all, and, with any luck, maybe it's not too late to help him, even in prison. That's all we can hope for."

After breakfast, they walked around a bit, just to burn off some nervous energy. They thought about taking a small trip to The Strip to see what all of the hype was about, but try as they might, there was nothing further from their minds. Peace and quiet was more their speed, and the more relaxed they could be, the better.

At a little past 11:00 a.m., they checked in with the police station to see if there was anything new to report. There was nothing.

Chapter 47

Zach disregarded the smart, calculated decision he had previously made and began to turn back west—the same direction from which he had come—heading straight back toward Las Vegas. Though he was wise beyond his years and had the heart of a killer, there was still a part of him, deep down, that needed to know the truth. He longed for answers. If it meant he needed to give up his life, then so be it. The life he had wasn't worth living anyway.

He wasn't suicidal by any means; quite the opposite. However, the truth was something he'd wondered about for as long as he could remember. This could all be a hoax, orchestrated by reporters with some superb imaging technology and an even better creative side to formulate a headline story, but somehow, he believed otherwise.

He took extra notice of the sights around him, relishing in his freedom as he had never done before. He wanted to drive for hours and think about what his next move would be. If there was any way he could find these two women without any police or surveillance and just get the answers he needed, he could then move on.

Once he got the truth, he could even make these two his last victims before he started to lie low for a while. The irony would be something the media would love and talk about for ages. A fifteen-year-old outsmarting and outrunning the law would go over real well.

Where were these officers when his alleged father's killer was out running loose all over town? If they would've caught him when they should've, his father would be alive and he'd have had the life that was rightfully his, instead of the shitty, abusive life that was so forcefully pushed upon him.

As he drove past the state line into Las Vegas, he pulled into a seedy pub and singled out his next victim. Killing was an addiction to him, similar to how cigarettes feed off of the lives of others.

He approached a middle-aged woman who wasn't attractive in the least and offered to buy her a drink. She had unkempt bleached hair, and wore chipped nail polish on her long, uneven fingernails and an outfit that didn't match in the least—pink stretch pants with a fluorescent green T-shirt. He didn't remember that look ever qualifying as a fashion statement.

He did his very best at pretending to flirt and make her feel desirable and special. "I don't know anybody in this town. Feel like going out for a little while for a day on the town?"

She gave him her best smile and accepted with pride. She did not even ask his name or offer any resistance. This was going to be easy.

He let her finish her drink, though how someone could drink and be more than halfway inebriated at 11:00 a.m. was a mystery to him. After she finished, Zach led her toward the front door and out toward his "borrowed" car.

She was already fairly intoxicated; he could only imagine how many drinks she had thrown down prior to his arrival. At least she wouldn't die of alcohol poisoning.

He drove a bit further. They were still fifty to sixty minutes from The Strip. Out this way, there were plenty of hiking trails and an abundance of desert. It was bright and sunny, but this might be his last hoorah for a while. It was going to be well worth the risk.

"*So, where ya from? Have you lived in Nevada your whole life?*" She tried to act and speak like a normal, decent citizen but slurred every word so that it sounded more like, "*So, where ya fra? Ha you lib in Neva your ho li?*"

He guessed that at this point, he still had to play Mr. Nice Guy and pretend to be interested in anything that this unknowing loser had to say. "Am I from Nevada? Yes. Born and raised. How about yourself?" He was trying to sound animated, perhaps even a little witty. All the while, he was just looking for a good place to pull over and put her and her hideous getup out of their misery.

"*Oh, me? I've lived all over the place. I only moved here recently.*" She again slurred her words and sounded ridiculous. It was almost painful. Thankfully, Zach saw a nice, remote area coming up on his right. A dirt road was just what he was looking for.

Not many people in their right minds go wandering down dirt roads. If they are smart, they have seen all of the horror films where only a homicidal maniac would be waiting for them at the end. For those who hadn't been to a movie in a while, they usually stayed away just to avoid ruining the tread on their tires.

Not Zach. He didn't care one ounce about the tread on his tires, and lucky for him, he *was* the homicidal maniac.

Since this wasn't *his* car, he didn't have any of his weapons with him. This one was going to be a bit more challenging. But hey, challenging can be fun.

He looked around the car for something he could use. Not too many of the typically desired killing instruments in an old lady's vehicle, but then there it was, right in front of him—a nice, heavy-duty, plastic bag. This would work out just perfectly. He sometimes marveled at how resourceful he was.

"*Where are we goin'? Doesn't look like anythin' excitin' goin' on down there.*" She was annoying him now. She didn't put the ending "g" on any of her words. How did people like this exist?

"Oh, honey. Don't go worrying your pretty little smile about it. There's plenty to do down there. Just wait and see."

She looked at him with a slight amount of awareness now. Some intelligence seemed to flash in her eyes for a brief moment but dissipated just as quickly. She then smiled and said, "*Oh, OK. You learn somethin' new every day.*"

"Some people do. Unfortunately, you're just not one of them," Zach said as he pulled off onto a nice, quiet, remote spot. No signs of tire tracks; no signs of people. It was perfect.

She looked at him now, a trickle of light flowing through her eyes with some recognition of danger, but without the fast reflexes to pull her out of this ominous situation safely.

"How would you like to go for a walk?"

"*Uh, I think we better be headin' back into town. I don't like this place. Gives me the creeps. Reminds me of one of those films; ya know, where those poor people get hacked into little pieces by a masked, crazy lunatic.*"

"Well, town is a little bit far from here. I think we should go for a walk. I don't see any masked men around, do you?" He felt a little bad about his decision to kill her. Normally, he only killed someone if they did something wrong to him. This woman hadn't done anything wrong other than speak in an annoying, uneducated manner. He bet she had never read a book in her life. That was good enough for him, though.

Beggars couldn't be choosers, and right now, he didn't have enough time to be selective on whom his next victim would be. He grabbed the scrunched up plastic bag and walked around the car to the passenger's side door. He opened it and gently pulled on her arm. Then, when she offered the least bit of resistance, he found that he needed to use a bit more force.

"Hey, let go of me," she stammered. *"I can get out of the car myself. Don't need no man pullin' me in directions I don't wanna go."*

That was it. He was getting irritated now. He had almost considered letting her live, but her loud voice, coupled with speaking like an imbecile, made it easy to dispose of her.

She tried to put up a struggle, but having a morning breakfast consisting of straight alcohol did not exactly work in her favor. She could barely stand up straight to keep her balance, and being drunk and dehydrated did not exactly improve the situation.

She wasn't quite yet grasping the dire circumstance that she was in at the moment, but sooner than later, realization would set in. She looked around at her surroundings, but out in the desert, everything starts to look the same.

She then noted Zach snapping the plastic bag open but had no concept of its relevance.

"Lady, you must've had a difficult life. I mean, it's obvious that you've never even looked in the mirror; otherwise, you'd never leave your house like that. Secondly, drinking before noon? I can tell this is a daily ritual with you.

"I consider myself to be a fair guy. I always think of what's best for everyone, and I like to be generous and take charge.

"I have brought with me today a gift, just for you. You may not be able to thank me now, but you will be thankful." He held the plastic bag by the handles, fidgeting with it, opening it and closing it, and looking inside like there was some treasure in there.

"Do you know what this is?"

"Of course, I do. It's a shoppin' bag."

"Right. It is a shopping bag. Have you ever noticed the many uses of your typical supermarket *shoppin'* bag?"

She couldn't quite grasp what he was saying. She answered his questions as though she was a student following a teacher's directives. *"You can use it as a trash bag."*

"Good! That's very good. You can certainly use it as a trash bag. You can also use it to asphyxiate someone."

She looked at him with a painted on blank stare. He purposely used big words like "asphyxiate," as he knew she wouldn't understand their meaning. This was getting to be fun.

"As…what? What was that word you said?"

"Asphyxiate. Do you know what that means?"

She shook her head no.

"Here, let me show you." He reached for her hand and gently led her toward him. He flashed his notorious, beautiful smile and immediately made her believe he was leaning in to kiss her. He put his arm around her and moved his body in closer. He lowered his mouth to hers, taking in the disgusting scent of stale cigarettes and alcohol. As she looked up to bring her mouth to his, she moved her body yet closer and closed her eyes, bracing herself for the kiss of a lifetime.

At that same moment, Zach took the plastic bag and, instead of kissing her, tossed the bag over her head and tightly held the base of it closed, grasping the handles.

Her eyes popped open, and he could still see her, though not as clearly through the plastic. He tilted his head and just stared into her eyes with a slight grin.

She fell underneath him and tried her best to release his grip, but he was way too strong. Her best efforts were nothing compared to Zach's incredible strength. She tried to scream, which only made matters worse for her, pulling the plastic in closer to her mouth, suffocating her more quickly. He really didn't care how long it took. He wasn't in a rush, not yet anyway.

He stood like a statue while she clumsily pulled and punched. It would all be over soon. After about four minutes, she fell all the way to the ground, eyes wide open, painted with fear. He didn't bother to close them for her. He was disgusted and didn't want to get any closer to her than necessary.

Zach felt more alive than ever. This had been his easiest kill yet. The best part was that he didn't need to move her body, nor walk two miles. His car was right in front of him, and they were already far enough into Nowhere's Land that it might be days before they found her, if ever. With any luck, the scavengers of the desert would come and remove the body. They were always willing to assist.

He removed the plastic bag, otherwise known as evidence, and took it with him in the car. He would throw it out the window a few miles closer to Vegas. At least they wouldn't pin this murder on him. Of course, they could match hair and fibers in the car against the victim, but he would be sure to get a new car in good time.

He took one last look at this pathetic woman, and, before getting back in the car, he decided to steal her credit card. He might need it for his plan to work. He started the engine, turned on the radio, and began to belt out some tunes.

His first stop would be the local convenience store to pick up a newspaper. He wanted to see if there were any clues about where his newly discovered relatives may be.

If he couldn't find them, he would have no choice but to turn himself in, but he would give it his all. Jail was the last place he opted to visit.

Chapter 48

Alex and Amber were getting antsy. Surely someone from the police station would call them soon. There had to be some type of lead, didn't there?

How could they let a murderer, much less a fifteen-year-old murderer, evade them to the point where they didn't even have a possible trail.

Alex began having second thoughts. What were the odds that this was indeed her son? Wouldn't it be more likely that her son died fourteen years ago at the hands of an alleged psychopath?

There had to be people all over the world who shared the same features of Amber and herself. Yes, it was true that this Zach person also had the same exact bone structure as Jack, but it could also quite conceivably be a coincidence.

What if this was all for nothing? What if they'd wasted all of their money on a trip and sent the officers, news team, and the entire city of Las Vegas on a wild goose chase for a kid that might not even be related. Last night's newscast would then be another waste of taxpayers' money, not to mention the media and the community's time and efforts that could be otherwise used in a more efficient manner.

She had to wipe that thought from her head. As ironic and impossible as it was, there were things that inexplicably pointed to Zach being her son. First and foremost were Amber's dreams. Amber said the person in her dreams closely resembled Zach/Kevin, almost to perfection. Second, Steve's dead body had been found in Las Vegas. Third, the age of Zach and his unmistakable eyes matched those of her one-year-old baby.

"Amber, let's go to the police station again today. I have an idea."

"What more can we do, Mom? He's not just going to come see us like we're having a happy family dinner and we just invited him. It's not going to be that easy. He may never show his face again. We have to realize that."

"You know, sometimes you have the same mindset as a sixty-year-old woman," Alex said, clearly annoyed. "I understand that, Amber, and I do realize that every move we make is nothing short of taking chances. As long as we take charge of the situation, however, we might be able to yield some results. I think we should give our location. Let him know where we are. Regardless of his possible relation to us, I'm sure he is a smart individual who does not want to be cornered by the Las Vegas police department.

"If we can somehow lure him to a location and meet with him, we can get the answers we need and possibly get him some help. He'll never be a free man, but perhaps he'll be a reformed one and no more innocent people will have to die at the hands of my son, if he is my son."

"Sorry, Mom. One of us has to be logical. I want to help him too, but he may be too far gone. They estimate that he has killed people numbering into the double digits. If that is the case, what makes you think he's going to spare us?

"He has no loyalty to us. For all we know, he may even blame you for his kidnapping and resent me for surviving that night with not so much as a scratch. You have to come to terms with that. If you don't, you are going to be harshly disappointed. Do you get that, Mom? Please tell me you do."

"I get it, Amber. Now, I'm going to the police station. Are you coming?"

Amber made a noise that resembled a growl and, nursed a nauseas pang before following her unrelenting mother to the bona fide lion's den, otherwise known as the Las Vegas Police Station.

Alex made her new thoughts known to the captain of the police force. He didn't think it was a good idea, but, with Alex's persuasive qualities, he was swayed.

On the evening news program, they would show Alex and Amber "caught "off guard" in a popular restaurant off of The Strip, right outside their hotel. The newscaster would hold a supposed impromptu interview, where it would be announced that Alex and Amber were hoping Zach would turn himself in. It would also show the awning of the Bella Luna, as a teaser for Zach to come looking there for them.

They prayed that this would go off without a hitch, only later thinking of the consequences that could occur if it did not.

Never once during the planning of this sneaky façade did Alex or Amber seriously think anything could go wrong. Why would it? They had the planning and backup from the Las Vegas Police Department. Even though they had lost Zach once, what were the chances that it could possibly happen again?

Their night was to begin at 7:00 p.m. at Angelo's Italian Restaurant, which was situated right outside the hotel's doors. The news team made sure to videotape them walking into the restaurant, clearly focusing on the brightly lit Bella Luna sign. They had no reason to believe that Zach was even watching, or if he was, that he would even be interested.

Even if he didn't watch this tonight, it was sure to be on the cover of every newspaper in Las Vegas circulation. Surely he would want to pick one up. It was unheard of for a nearly convicted serial killer to *not* be narcissistic. They were usually quite interested in what the media and community had to say about them.

There were to be plainclothes police officers guarding every corner of the hotel, along with two trailing not far behind Alex and Amber no matter where they went.

The impromptu interview was a good one at first; very enticing.

"So, Mrs. Rider, what do you hope to accomplish if you see your son? Do you think he's guilty? What if he's convicted? Is there anything you want to say to the family of the victims? Is there anything you want to say to Zach?" The questions went on and on. They were supposed to keep it clean, and not take any cheap shots at Alex and Amber, but they were reporters first and human second.

They wanted to make a blockbuster story, first and foremost, so they weren't exactly gentle in their line of questioning. Alex shot them some dagger glances as they attacked her family. Even though her son was being accused of murder, he was still her baby whose life was stolen from him. Her heart still ached for him, regardless of his alleged crimes.

The last straw was the reporter's final question. "So, Mrs. Rider, if your son was kidnapped from you fourteen long years ago, snatched from the very arms you held him in, how is it that today, you are ready to put him in front of the firing line and risk a life of imprisonment, taking away the very freedom you so badly wanted him to have. How does a mother turn her own baby in? I'm sure the public would want to know the answer to this."

She nearly slapped him in the face for that one. Now the entire nation had heard that question and would be thinking the same thing. Unfortunately, Zach was part of the nation and would now be thinking his own mother wanted him in jail. Now she had to give an answer. She couldn't just leave like she had initially wanted to.

"Your question is rude and ridiculous. You ask how I could turn in my own son? That's not what I'm doing. I want to see my son and explain his life to him. Let him know what happened fourteen years ago. Help him understand that he was loved, is *still* loved, and that we want to help him in any way possible.

"Kevin living a life on the run is not safe for him and is a surefire way to have his life cut short. With our help, he can get rehabilitated. Without it, he can be killed. And although he is my son, I don't want other innocent people to die if he is indeed guilty. If perhaps he understands how his life turned out the way it did, his anger may slowly dissipate and people's lives may be saved in the interim.

"Now, if you'll excuse me from your destructive questions, this interview is now over with. I hope you never need to make an important decision, one where the outcome of people's lives is held in the balance. God bless us all if that should happen."

With that, both she and Amber stormed out of the restaurant without looking back.

Alex knew she would definitely have some deep-rooted issues to deal with when it was confirmed that this was in fact Kevin. She wasn't oblivious to that fact. Somehow, it seemed that if she could speak to him and just let him know what had happened, he would be on his way to healing. That thought might be naïve, but it was what kept her strong.

If she didn't have that theory to hold on to, then all had been lost, once again. Hopefully, Zach would step forward and at least be a little intrigued. Even though he was being accused of dreadful crimes, that didn't guarantee that he was necessarily void of *any* heart and soul. They hoped there was still at least some shred of decency in him.

Chapter 49

Zach walked into the most repulsive convenience store, run by people who probably couldn't even read. This was exactly what he was seeking. The less people noticed about him, the better off he was. He had never actually been on the run before, but even he knew that he had to stay disguised, inconspicuous, and completely low-key.

There it was on the headlines of the *Oasis Daily News*. "Zach Jacobs: A Happy Family Reunion?"

He had to hand it to the reporters; they knew how to put a sick and twisted spin on information. He made a mental note of the reporter's name, just in case he ever got the opportunity to have some quality "alone" time with him.

The headline made him so angry, like his life was just some sort of joke. "Probably some sick-looking, scrawny guy who I could take down in a minute." He said this out loud, but low enough so that it only seemed like he was mumbling. The store clerk cocked his head a bit—sort of like a dog trying to understand the human language—then went back to organizing the gum rack.

Zach bought a large soda with lots of ice and ventured back to his car. He drove about three miles and pulled over in a supermarket parking lot so he could read the news in private while enjoying the shade of a large palm tree.

The name of the restaurant was Angelo's, and the name of the hotel couldn't be missed—"The Bella Luna." He wondered if that was where they were staying. The article didn't mention anything of their whereabouts while on this trip, but it did tell of how they only wanted to find him, talk to him, tell him the truth of what had happened, and lastly, help him.

What heartfelt thoughts. Where were you the rest of my life? The cops said I was missing, and you just gave up? Just said OK and accepted it without putting up a fight or sending out another search team, huh? Let me live a life of misery? Though no one was around, he felt the need to express his thoughts out loud. He was accustomed to talking only to himself, as it wasn't like he had many friends to share his heartfelt emotions with.

He'd feel better once he spoke to them. The newspaper article and news broadcast was a trap. Zach was well aware of that fact, but his anger was real and here to stay. He wanted to address his issues with good old Mom and meet his lucky sister. Amber was her name. How was it that Amber got to live the life of luxury while he ate coyotes and insects just to survive?

He was going to that hotel today, but he had to be smart. Cops were going to be circulating the area; he knew how this worked. They were all going to be on the lookout for a fifteen-year-old male in a car that was already reported stolen.

They weren't looking for a female though, and definitely not one showing up in a limousine. This was going to be fun. Mom, meet your daughter, Helena Short.

The first place he needed to stop was downtown Las Vegas, where tons of kiosks sold all types of flashy items or gimmicks with no questions asked. He picked up a few good bits and pieces and was well on his way to a transformation. One of his shopping bags held tons of makeup, from foundation to mascara and a lightly-colored lipstick. He wanted to be disguised, not look ridiculous. That would just draw more attention.

In his second shopping bag—a women's blouse and purse. Though he knew he'd be uncomfortable, he also bought some girly jeans and high-heeled shoes. His last stop was a wig boutique, where he bought a long, brunette wig that had been styled to look soft and flowing. He looked neither elegant nor stylish, which was just perfect for what he needed to do.

He was confident he would be able to pull this off without a hitch. He got changed in his car, put on his makeup, and arranged his wig perfectly with bobby pins so that it wouldn't fall off.

When he was done, he walked into a novelty store and admired his new look in one of the full-length mirrors. *Wow. I do look good if I say so myself.*

Next, he walked to the nearest payphone, which wasn't easy to find now that most people owned cell phones. He spotted one on the far corner, deposited a few coins, and dialed information. "Limousine service for Las Vegas, Nevada please."

The operator on the other end named a few places, and Zach selected the second one—"Merle's Luxury Limousines."

He asked to be picked up outside of one of the nicer hotels located on The Strip, to make it look like he was actually vacationing there. His plan was to drive a few blocks, park on a desolate side road, and take a cab to the hotel. From there, he would take the limousine to the Bella Luna.

What would happen next remained to be seen. Zach wasn't one of those people who believed in fate and destiny. Tonight, he was going to be responsible for his own circumstances and get the long-awaited answers he so greatly desired. The night was all his, and nighttime was something he loved.

Chapter 50

"Good evening, ma'am. Your destination please?"

"The Bella Luna, please," Zach said, amazed that even his voice was somewhat believable. He was proud of himself.

"Night on the town, ma'am?"

"I'm sorry. I've a bit of laryngitis. Please excuse me if I can't talk too much," he said, smiling sweetly. Zach didn't want to give out too much information, just in case he slipped up. He was running on adrenalin right now and was anxious to hear all about his life story, or what should've been his life story.

He hadn't yet decided whether he would let his family live. It would be much more fun disposing of them too.

"No problem. Will you need my services later in the evening, or shall I leave once we arrive at the Bella Luna, Miss…"

"Short. Helena Short. That will be all, so you can leave."

They arrived at the beautiful but quaint hotel. As they pulled into the outside registration area, they were surrounded by faux green grass, waterfalls, numerous varieties of colorful flowers, and tons of large palm trees.

Bellhops arrived at the door of the limousine within mere seconds and assisted Miss Short out of the car. Zach paid the limo driver, tipped the bellhop, and made his way into the hotel, glancing at the very restaurant his mother and sister had dined at the previous evening.

He registered a room and paid in full with cash, leaving his most recent kill's credit card as a deposit for any damages. He was certain no one was going to report her missing for a long while. Zach only hoped someone like her had a balance left to use. He cringed as they ran it through. "Thank you, Helena. Enjoy your stay."

"Thank you!"

He went to his room, checked his makeup, and relaxed on the bed for a few moments. After about an hour, he went back down and made an effort to appear confused. He glanced at the hotel front desk and was glad to see that the night shift had come and relieved the day shift. No one would recognize him. He walked right up to the friendly looking man behind the counter, a tall fellow with broad shoulders. One a girl might even find handsome.

"Good evening, ma'am. How may I assist you today?"

"I feel kind of silly, but I was so excited to check out the hotel grounds and swimming pool, I, uh, forgot my room number. I have my key here, but just completely forgot my room number." In his girlish costume, Zach flashed the key, smiled innocently, and tried to appear flirty as well.

"Sure. I can look that up for you. Last name?"

"Rider. Amber Rider." With that, Zach just smiled some more. If this worked, he was definitely smarter than he thought, or just more conniving.

"Ms. Rider, your room number is 204. We hope you enjoy your stay."

A little flirting goes a long way. "Oh, thank you! I love it already. I'll be sure not to get lost again!" As he said the words, he went back to his room, but not before first taking a stroll down the hallway of the second floor. He paused briefly by room 204, long enough to hear talking from within the room, but not long enough for anyone to notice, should there be cameras watching.

He had resisted the urge to knock on the door and barge his way in. If he wanted to avoid getting caught and arrested, he had to play this the right way. He wanted to wait long enough for them to get discouraged and then make his move. A few more hours until morning was all he needed. This was going to work out just fine.

He went back to his room, lay down on the bed, and stared at the view of the mountains outside his hotel window. The sun was going down, and the clock read 7:00 p.m. This was by far the most luxurious place he had ever stayed in. As a matter of fact, he had never stayed in any type of hotel, nice or otherwise.

He figured he had a busy couple of days and should get to sleep early. Tomorrow was going to be the day, and he needed to be well rested. He chucked as he thanked Helena Short for the room and thought she must've been partly eaten already by the wildlife that roamed that lonely desert.

By morning, her body would be torn to shreds, he was sure. Only the fragments of her clothing remained, and those would be dragged, along with her body, by the coyote that stumbled upon her. Coyotes usually prefer to do the killing themselves, but in an area as desolate as the desert, they sometimes have to take what they can get.

Or perhaps a vulture would be lucky enough to find the body and use it for a nice meal. Scavengers by nature, vultures thrived on these golden opportunities. They may even use portions of the clothes to build a thrifty, colorful type of nest. He felt safe with this kill. He felt he was helping the rest of nature survive, if only for a few days.

He went to bed thinking only positive thoughts, feeling quite at ease with himself, and enjoying the first-time comforts of a firm bed with plush pillows and soft blankets. *I could get used to this.*

He looked at the clock. It was now 7:30. He closed his eyes and fell fast asleep, setting his internal clock for 5:00 a.m. He was going to need to get up early to make sure his plan could be carried out without exception.

Aside from the mild humming of the air conditioner and the occasional voices that trailed in the hallway, the hotel was incredibly quiet. Noise normally didn't affect Zach, as he was quite comfortable catching some sleep anywhere, especially within the confines of nature, where there was no such thing as perpetual quiet.

Tonight, however, he not only welcomed the serene environment, he embraced it. He was already on his way to a getting a long overdue good night's sleep.

Chapter 51

The sun started its early rise and shed enough light for Zach to wake up without the assistance of an obnoxious alarm clock. Never having the need or want for an alarm, Zach always relied upon his own internal clock to wake him if need be. He never had to adhere to a set schedule that required him to be anywhere early. His part-time jobs always started either mid-morning or over the graveyard shift. Either way, he was already awake and prepared for his day.

He woke up, showered, and got dressed in his "Helena Short" outfit, though he swore he looked much better than she ever did. After carefully applying his makeup and wig, he took one last glance in the mirror, blew himself a kiss, and headed out of the room, making sure to hang the "Do Not Disturb" sign on the back of the hotel room door. He didn't need housekeeping rummaging through his belongings, though there were only a few.

He made his way to the hotel business center, where there were a couple of computers, printers, and some books for the intellectual traveler. He glanced through all of the books and grabbed one he had never read before. It was now 5:30, and the rest of the hotel must have still been asleep, most likely overcoming a strong hangover. Apparently people who visited Vegas thought it was a law that they must drink themselves into oblivion.

Around the corner from the business center, a small café served coffee, pastries, bagels, and some egg sandwiches. He placed his order at the counter for a bacon, egg, and cheese sandwich along with a large cola. Not drawing too much attention to himself, he walked back to one of the couches in the lobby and situated himself there to enjoy his breakfast and his book. At least that is how he wanted it to appear to the rest of the hotel's guests and staff.

There was another older man there doing precisely the same thing, so "Helena" didn't look like an outcast. He smiled shyly at the older man and then sat by himself, hoping his wig was still in place. He took the compact out of his purse and ensured that it was. He was sliding easily into the role of Helena and was anxious to get the day started on its fated plan. Patience was the key element for success at this point, so Zach took his time eating his breakfast while at the same time taking notice of any guests walking in or out of the hotel.

By 8:30, Zach was halfway through the book he had selected, making sure to keep one eye on the lookout for anyone resembling his "relatives" who had appeared in the paper. He was starting to lose patience, thinking his family members were late risers and not conforming to his early schedule.

Just as he was about to get up and use the restroom, he spotted them making their way toward the entryway of the hotel and sort of jumped. Timing was now of the essence. He figured housekeeping would be entering their hotel room within a half hour to an hour, so he slowly got up and pushed the up button on the elevator to go to the second floor.

The housekeeping carts were out, and Zach watched as the maids spoke Spanish to each other, catching only every other word. Zach had taught himself Spanish by reading a few text books. He wasn't proficient, but he knew enough to get by if the need should ever arise.

Lucky for him, they were just finishing up room 208. A few more rooms to clean and they would be starting room 204. Zach took the elevator to his own room and went into his bag for some additional items.

He made sure to bring a sharp-edged knife with him this time and a gag, just in case, though he really didn't want them to stop talking. He wanted to hear the whole entire story, from start to finish. The remainder of their lives would be held in the balance, dependent upon how well Zach believed and/or liked their story.

He took his time getting back to the second floor, even using the stairs instead of the elevator to prolong his arrival a little more. He strolled down the hallway, almost as if he were taking in the scenery, and paused by room 204. He couldn't have timed it any better. The maid was just finishing up.

As he approached the doorway, she noticed him and smiled. Zach, still dressed as Helena Short, smiled back of course and asked if she were done. She said yes, and Zach walked in, claiming the room to be his. Zach put down his things as if he belonged there, checking his reflection in the mirror to make it appear that he was completely relaxed. This worked like a charm; the maid didn't question it. Why would she?

Zach handed her a five dollar tip. Not too much to draw attention, but enough to keep her happy. She shut the door on her way out, and Zach took off his high heels and changed into sneakers before making himself comfortable on the bed. Now all he had to do was be patient. Perhaps Alex and Amber went to breakfast or for a morning stroll.

It was possible they went shopping for a few hours, so he would have to just sit tight until that door opened. Then, his lifelong quest of knowing exactly who he was would be over. No cops were involved; no media to speak of. Once he got what he needed, he would slip away into the night, unnoticed and fast enough that no police would be on his trail.

Chapter 52

Alex and Amber made their way to breakfast, both feeling more anxiety and stress than they ever dreamed possible. The interview they so meticulously planned hadn't worked out the way they had hoped. The reporter asked questions that were way out of line, focusing on negative points for everyone involved instead of doing what he was paid to do: Get Zach's interest and bring him in.

Today, they needed some comic relief and some normalcy.

"Feel like shopping a little, or maybe going to see a show today, Amber? I hear they have some great afternoon comedy acts. The police have our cell phone numbers should any new information arise. What do you think? Or, how about some sightseeing? We can go to the Hoover Dam on one of those bus tours."

"Hmm, you know what, Mom? Let's do it. Let's go sightseeing. I can't take much more of this anyway. I am about to go insane. I have to get my purse, though. I left it in the room. Mind going back?"

"Not at all. Let's go!"

"What time does the bus leave?" Amber asked as they headed toward their room.

"I think there's one bus that leaves the hotel at 12:00 p.m. and one at 2:00 p.m. We should have plenty of time. We'll be gone for most of the day, so bring whatever you think you will need. Do you have your key?"

"Um, let me check. Yep, right here." She slipped the card key into the hotel room lock. Zach heard his cue faster than he thought he would and was pleased. He hopped off of the bed, quickly straightening the bedspread, and slid underneath it.

"Mom, do you see my purse anywhere? I could swear I left it right here on the dresser."

Zach had moved their necessary belongings into the bathroom so that he could make his move without them noticing. Alex and Amber both searched for it, making their way into the large bathroom. "Here it is, honey."

With that, Zach got out from underneath the bed, still in his wig and makeup, and waited for them to come back out of the bathroom. He had hoped they wouldn't scream and had a plan to say he was housekeeping if they did.

"OK, let's go," Alex said. "Whoa! Who are you? I didn't hear you come in."

Zach smiled. They didn't scream. "You mean you don't recognize me?"

Alex spoke first. "I'm sorry, should I? Do you work here?" She didn't feel the least bit threatened at first, not even thinking of the possibility, and then, like a light switch, it clicked that something wasn't right. In fact, something was completely wrong. Her senses were all now fully aware of the impending danger that stood before her.

Zach just smiled and shook his head. As he did so, he began to pull off his wig and pulled out his knife at the same time. "Scream, and you will both die. Stay quiet, and you may actually live."

"Kevin?" Alex whispered, her voice quivering.

"Did you just call me Kevin? I'm sure you made a mistake." He locked eyes with Amber and couldn't help but see his own features mirrored in her face. He didn't want to believe them just yet. It was too soon to tell if they were legit or just some crazy psychos wanting a piece of the action. This was Las Vegas, after all.

Quiet and confusion filled the room. Alex spoke first, calmly and in her usual soft voice. "Kevin, don't do this.

Please don't do anything rash. Let us explain. We can work this all out, get you some help. You must believe us. Listen, at any point during your life, did you ever have parents or a guardian?"

"During any point of my life?" he repeated. "Do you call this a life? No. Not that I know of. Why? You looking to adopt?"

She brushed off that question and looked toward her purse. "Let me get just one thing for you. I'm not trying anything funny; I promise."

He let her go into her purse, and she pulled out something. She then asked, "Do you know this man?" She flashed the picture of her husband's killer and son's captor.

The corners of Zach's jaw began to tighten, and he looked up at Alex. He read the article from fourteen years ago, first skimming it and then reading it in greater detail. *This* article wasn't shown on the news. He wasn't expecting to read the entire story.

"Lady, is this some kind of a joke? As you can see, I'm not the joking type. You're in Vegas. You should've gone to a comedy club if you're looking for a good laugh. Didn't you pick up any brochures when you landed?"

She trembled as she looked at her son and wanted to hug him and let him cry on her shoulder. She wanted to make up for fourteen years of misery that he had to endure and explain how she couldn't find him, how she tried the best that she could, but she was led to believe he was dead.

She wanted to do all that, but she couldn't. Across from her was a boy about to be convicted if caught for horrendous and gruesome murders that had occurred over at least the past three years.

She whispered, "No joke. You are my son. And this is your twin sister, Amber." She added, more quietly now, "Your name is Kevin." She was trembling. Though this was her son, and she was sure of that now, she feared him. Life had made him almost inhuman, except that he was human once. And he was beautiful and lovable.

He looked at her and then looked toward the door. Though he heard no sounds in the hallway, he was starting to get a bit paranoid. He wanted to believe this was true. As much of a hardened criminal as he was, he longed for the affection and tenderness of a loving parent. He wanted to refute her and his newly found sister, but even he couldn't deny the uncanny resemblance. It was plain as day. You'd have to be blind not to notice it.

"My name's Zach. I wanted to take this opportunity to make this clear to you, so that you'll stop making appearances claiming to be my family. If you really want to get into my mind, you're asking for trouble. I'm doing my best at giving you an out, once and for all. Do you *understand*?"

Alex and Amber both wiped away tears from the corners of their eyes as Zach focused on a wad of gum sticking to the wall. He couldn't scream. He couldn't cry. Not now. Never again.

While swallowing back years of pent-up tears, Alex closed with, "Kevin, I only hope you can accept my help. I want to do what I can. It's not your fault. Steve was a terrible person and made you that way. You were loved by all of us. We can never change your life or who you are or what you have done, but we *can* help with whatever you need. You can change your future."

He wanted to run. He needed to get out. He was now like a rabid, caged animal that needed to be free. He needed to kill. He wanted to lash out at the two audacious women who stood before him. How dare they interrupt his comfortable life of solitude? He was fine being who he was. The reality of their story had started to set in, and thoughts of killing them rushed through his head like a freight train traveling at full speed.

He glared at them with eyes full of darkness, full of fourteen years of immense inner pain, and made one final request. "I gave you fair warning, yet you still stand before me. I am telling you to leave your room now, yet you have ignored my request. Have it your way.

"My name, as I know it, is Zach. You're now telling me my name is Kevin, and my father's name was Jack. I want to hear the entire story right now. Don't leave anything out. Don't try to be a hero and get the police involved. That would be one of the biggest mistakes you could possibly make."

He sat on the edge of the bed, surprisingly relaxed as he belted out his orders.

"First, you need to call your friends at the police station and check in. Act like you are searching for information. I know you thought you were keen in staging that interview, as if it weren't supposed to take place, except that I know better. I'm pretty smart for a fifteen-year-old. That should be a direct compliment to you, if I am, in fact, your son.

"Call and act as if you are annoyed with the system and ask if they have found any information yet. Once they say no, politely tell them you'll check back later. No tricks. I may let you live. If I feel as if you are trying to get me arrested, I will kill you the second you hang up the phone, and I still won't get caught."

Alex obeyed him—except for one small detail. The police had advised her that she was putting both herself and Amber on the spot and that they should have alternate plans if something should go awry.

They explained that if they were *alone* and called the police station, she would spell her last name *incorrectly*. If she were to ever call in because she was in trouble, she should spell her last name *correctly*. This would be a clear indication that she was in trouble, and the call would be traced immediately to get a location. Zach wouldn't be the wiser, expecting her to spell her name the correct way.

He motioned for her to hang up, and she did so without question. Her heart broke for what she had just done, but it would help him in the long run. There was no good choice right now, but not turning him in meant he would go back and kill again, and possibly get killed himself. She wanted to take the lesser of the two evils, and unfortunately, turning in her son was the one that prevailed.

Amber stared on in silence, daydreaming if only for a minute of what her life would've been like had she known about her brother, or better yet, if he had never been kidnapped. She shook her head to snap herself out of it and get back into reality, which was that she was locked inside a hotel room with a serial killer who just happened to be her long-lost twin brother.

"So, what happened? You lost me? At a year old, you just let some random guy kidnap me and took the cops' word for it that I was already dead, huh?" he asked dryly. "How is it that my beloved twin sister managed to survive without so much as a scratch? Luck, I suppose?"

"Kevin,"

"It's Zach."

Alex let out an exasperated sigh. "Zach, that's not how it went." She and Amber sat next to each other on the other bed.

"Well, I'm waiting. I am a pretty patient person, but come on, fifteen years of waiting is enough, don't ya think? Is that right? Am I fifteen? I don't even know when my birthday is. Amber, you should be able to tell me that, huh?"

"Yes, it is July 18, 1992. You're fifteen, just like me."

"Well, not exactly like you, right? I mean, you didn't try to escape the hands of a man who abused you every single day, did you? You didn't then push that same man down a flight of stairs by accident, but by luck find that he was dead, did you? Hmm, you didn't have to find creative ways to survive on a daily basis and get driven to the point of murder to deal with your frustrations, did you?

"So, please don't ever use the term 'just like me' when you are making idle comparisons between us. I'm nothing like you, aside from perhaps a small resemblance."

"No, Zach. No to all of those things. Can you please listen to what my mother, I mean our mother, has to say?"

"Please, by all means."

"Zach, fourteen years ago, your father and I had just returned home from an evening out, and you and Amber were in your cribs. Amber was fast asleep, but you were fussing terribly. The only way to ever calm you down was to hold you, and that's exactly what I did. I brought you out into the warm, fresh air and the three of us—your father, you, and I—sat on the porch.

"It was a gorgeous night. We had no clue Steve was responsible for previous murders. There was speculation, but no proof. He worked with your father.

"He approached us on foot, and we assumed that he lived in the area. He started talking small talk, and then it progressed to full-fledged gibberish. He wasn't making sense, to us anyway, and we got up to go inside and get away from him.

"What happened after that, Zach, was a complete blank. I saw him reach in his pocket, and I shielded you with my body. He shot your father."

Alex paused to regain her composure and swallow back the tears. "Your father died instantly. Steve then shot me. I don't recall anything after that, as I was unconscious.

"I woke up in the hospital to find your father was dead and you were missing. I couldn't leave the hospital. I tried to get up, tried to sneak away to find you, but I simply couldn't move. By the time I tried to find you, it was too late. Steve was long gone, and so were you. No one had any leads. Nothing. I wanted nothing more than to find you, Zach. Nothing more in this world would've made me any happier."

He started clapping. "That was a stellar performance, Mum. Did you rehearse that? It was absolutely beautiful, touching. I'm thoroughly impressed. Please tell me, is it here that we are all supposed to take part in a group hug? Should we reclaim our family bond and unite as one? How does this work? What is it that you expected to accomplish? Do you actually think you can change me, make me into a respectable man?

"Here's the hard truth. Whether you choose to believe me or not is up to you. I've killed a total of ten, maybe even eleven people. I enjoyed every single, blood-shedding minute of it. Similar to the way you enjoy eating, or breathing for that matter, I enjoy killing.

"I'm not about to give it up because you made a trip to Las Vegas to tell me your sad sob story of a promising evening that went bad.

"Now, you've been straight with me, so I'm going to return the favor. I won't kill you just yet. I may not even kill you at all if you do exactly as I say. If you don't, I will find you and I will haunt your every day and night. I know your last name now, and I know that you live on Long Island. It's not that difficult to find people these days, especially with a little money. Do you understand me?" His voice was getting gruff and almost hoarse, partly due to anger, partly due to suppressed sadness and built-up emotions.

He stood up and grabbed his gags. Both Alex's and Amber's eyes widened in horror. Was this how it ended? Their own relative killing them?

Amber spoke first. "You don't have to do this. You really don't. Zach, we just wanted to help you. You have to believe that. It's not too late. There is rehabilitation. We can *help* you." She was pleading at this point.

Alex tried to talk some sense into him. "Zach, whatever you need, we'll take care of. Counseling, lawyers, whatever it takes. You could still have a good life. There are programs in prison. Come on, we can *do* this!"

He looked them both in the eyes with a deadpan stare.

"I don't want your help. I don't want your pity. I'm going to leave this hotel room, and I'm going to gag you. I told you I'm not going to kill you, and I do keep my word. Like I said, do as I say, and you'll continue living your fruitful life, and I will continue robbing others of theirs.

"When the cops arrive, and I'm sure they will, don't describe me to them. Don't even tell them I was here. You'll figure out how to untie your gags and bindings. It shouldn't take you all too long. I should be an hour away by then in a direction you'll never know.

"If anything is leaked to the police, I'll know about it. Those boys can't keep anything off of the news. Have a nice life."

He actually felt moisture building up behind his eyelids. Were those tears? Anger and sadness had consumed him, and he need to fight some of it off quickly.

He gagged and bound his hostages and then went to check himself in the mirror. He rearranged his wig, fixed his makeup, and turned toward Alex and Amber. "Remember what I said. Sorry you came all this way, but hey, you can't change the world."

His voice was that of a cold-blooded murderer, but secretly, in his heart, he was sincere. The realization started to sink in that the two women sitting before him had done all that they could, but he had hardened his heart against the world and didn't want anyone to see how much he was hurting inside.

He turned toward the hotel door and pushed down on the lever to open it. As he did so, much to his surprise and dismay, he was greeted by two police officers, guns drawn, ready to kill. One officer rushed past him and untied the women.

Alex and Amber knew they would be there and watched as they read Zach his rights and handcuffed him. Tears streamed down their faces for a life that was given potential and stolen at such an early age.

Zach looked up at them, trying to figure out if they were to blame or if this was a chance meeting. He would find out. He hoped for their sakes they were not at fault.

Alex looked up, crying, watching as her son, whom she had just reunited with after fourteen years, was taken away in handcuffs.

All of the tension, all of the unknowing, anxiety, and regret, came flooding back at her faster than the speed of light. As she watched him get taken away, she sobbed uncontrollably. Amber looked on with tears in her eyes, but there was nothing she could do to console her mother.

Alex didn't even get to wrap her arms around her son and hold him like she had dreamed. His heart had been hardened, and rightfully so, and all she wanted to do now was just die. The last time she had looked in his eyes, he had looked at her like she was the only person who mattered in this world. He had complete and utter trust in her.

Now, there was nothing but blackness. It was not even hatred. It was just nothingness. And that was almost worse.

Chapter 53

Caught. Zach walked down the hallway of the hotel with his wrists tightly handcuffed behind his back. Given his previous track record of resisting arrest, these officers were not taking any chances. He tried to look over his shoulder for his beloved mother and newfound sister, but they were nowhere to be found.

He was alone once again. The promise of love and acceptance was taken away as quickly as it had been given. Their claim to want to help him was just a ploy to catch him, and now they could claim to be heroes and go on living their lives of luxury in their beautiful home on Long Island.

He was surprised to find that the police officers in charge were actually very respectful toward him. He expected them to be two inexperienced wise asses from the way they first appeared in the doorway. They even asked if his wrists were OK and if he was in pain, which he was not.

He actually felt numb. He wasn't in any physical pain, and mentally, he felt nothing. He thought that he should be upset, mad, sad, disappointed, relieved, but he felt no such emotions. His face held a stoic expression when he looked at his reflection as they passed a mirror in the hallway, and it perfectly matched the way he felt.

It was as if years of abuse, years of abusing others, had meant nothing. It felt as if his life was finally where it should be. Not that it was necessarily a good thing; it was just the right thing. He couldn't contribute any more to society than society could contribute to him.

What would he do now? Sit in a jail cell day after day, maybe read a few books over and over again and eat something that could maybe pass for food? To be honest, he cared more about the books than the food, as he was accustomed to eating whatever he could get his hands on, whether it be a juicy steak or the coyote that just crossed his path.

He was fine with the dreariness of the jail cell walls that he had seen time and time again on television. Being confined in a cell didn't even bother him all that much. But in prison, if you killed, you got punished for it. In the outside world, he was a professional—one who just made a few bad choices and got lazy.

As he walked, he closed his eyes and envisioned his first day in jail. The steel bars automatically unlocked, and the warden made an announcement: "Everyone to the cafeteria for breakfast, then half hour in the yard. After that, back to your cells. Any bullshit, you'll answer to me. Any questions, tough shit."

He would no longer have his freedom, and, of course, that was the one thing he couldn't live without. He had never in his semi-adult life had to obey an adult, boss or otherwise, and he didn't feel like he should have to start now.

Apparently, prison fights were common as well. He could definitely hold his own when prepared, but he realized there were men bigger and stronger than him. For those, he would have to outwit them; however, he wasn't planning on letting this get that far. He'd be out again; that was for sure. He just had to conjure up a way to make it happen.

The policemen made idle talk amongst themselves as they escorted Zach through the hallway, into the elevator, and down into the hotel garage where their police car was parked. No other policemen were around, as far as Zach could tell.

He shrugged off that feeling of dread almost as instantly as it came about. He'd most likely be dead in a few short days. He didn't necessarily want to die, but he didn't fear it either.

If that guy hadn't hit his bumper, Zach would still be sitting in his tiny but functional apartment, drinking a cola and reading a book or planning his next satisfying attack.

Getting nostalgic wasn't going to help him, though. He needed to either accept his fate, as he had read about millions of times, or he could create his own fate. Nothing in this life was impossible. Where there is a will, there's a way. You could do anything you set your mind to. Wasn't that a list of the inspirational clichés?

The policemen escorting him had been trained to be tough and to not take any bullshit. They had weapons and were instructed to use them if any sign of bad behavior should occur, or if anyone just got out of line.

Some men were stronger than Zach and could restrain him with zero effort. Others were stronger in strength but weaker in conviction. He surmised that the latter were the ones escorting him now. He remembered to smile at them, but not too much where he would look obnoxious or cunning; just enough to show ample respect.

He hadn't yet been deemed guilty. Hell, he hadn't even set foot in a jail cell yet. No sentence had been set before him. He began formulating a plan in his devious mind. One that might just work. It never hurt to try. What did he have to lose?

Chapter 54

Zach walked with his head low. Not like he was embarrassed, but as if he had regret.

If the men accompanying him spoke to him, he made it a point to have direct eye contact and speak softly, slowly, and with confidence but also respect. He asked them their names, knowing full well that if you address someone by name, it shows even greater respect.

The one cop on his left just looked at him with some suspicion when he asked, so he had to back it up some. "I just don't want to call you 'Hey you.' I find that to be rude. Is there a name you preferred to be addressed by?"

This pacified the cop a bit and he answered, "You can call me Officer Andrews."

"Thanks, Officer Andrews. I appreciate it." He took note of the possible amount of weapons they could have on them. He looked inconspicuously to his left and then to his right to measure up the size of their muscles the best he could. His mind kept talking to him: *"You have nothing to lose."*

He believed it, too. Prison would strip him of any type of life he did have, as pathetic as it may appear. It would only get worse. Death was better than what he had, and if it came to that, he would be OK with it. At least he gave it a try.

If he didn't get killed and had to go to prison, he could at least say he didn't go down without a fight. They wouldn't have ever caught him if he hadn't come back to Vegas on his own merit. It was his decision to learn about his life that brought him within the confines of their jurisdiction. Had he kept trekking east, he would have at least one more luscious kill under his belt, and probably one or two more stolen cars.

Zach felt pretty good about that. They only caught him because he let them. He got away once. There was no reason he couldn't get away again.

They were getting closer now to the police car. Zach could see the lights, now off, sitting atop the car. Tons of people walked toward the elevator from which they had just exited, each catching a quick stare at Zach, wondering what he could have done to have two police escorts. No one wanted to make eye contact, but curiosity was sometimes stronger than logic; that's what got him here.

He didn't mind. He understood the whole people watching thing. He was a professional at it. He had to be. It was him against the whole world, and he had to know what made people tick.

For instance, Officer Andrews had a slight limp. Not too noticeable unless you had been walking with him for twenty minutes. His neck was also hurting him, as he would stretch it every few minutes or so as though trying to get rid of a kink or two.

The officer on his right, Sergeant Denali, seemed to be in pretty good shape—lean and muscular, but with one slight imperfection. He wore glasses. He fidgeted with them often, leading Zach to assume that he usually wore contacts. Maybe today, his eyes were just not feeling right, or maybe he had an eye infection. Either way, today, he had chosen to wear glasses.

They got closer to the police car. *They shouldn't have parked so far. Guess they didn't have a choice.*

More families walked toward the elevator.

He had to be quick. Zach turned toward Sergeant Denali and head-butted him right in the eye, shattering his glasses and no doubt sending at least a few shards of glass into his eyes.

Officer Andrews went to get a better grip on Zach, and Zach kicked him in his bum leg and pushed him with as much force as possible with his hip. Officer Andrews went down, and as he did, Zach jumped on him, throwing force on the officer's neck, making sure to kink it even more. The officer was debilitated for about thirty seconds, while Sergeant Denali did his best to try to see clearly, being careful not to scratch his eyes even more.

Thirty seconds was all he needed. With his hands still bound behind his back, Zach made his way the best he could through mazes of parked cars. He jumped over obstacles as he made his way onto the lower level of the parking garage.

Though his balance was hindered, he was extremely fast; he even surprised himself with his own speed under the circumstances. He was almost there. He would be able to blend in with the public in no time—except for the handcuffs, but he'd find an alley and somehow work out a way to get them off.

He ran down the ramp of the parking garage; only two more floors to go. Zach skipped as many stairs as he could manage without falling flat on his face. He knew he could do it. Twice. Outsmarting and outrunning the cops twice. He was invincible. The bottom of his sneakers squeaked against the cement.

He had only one more floor to go. Almost there. By tonight, he would be on his way to live the life he was used to, the only life he had ever known, and that was just fine with him. He had the answers he had been seeking for most of his life and was happy to move on. A calming feeling of peace came over him, even though he was running for his life.

Then he felt it. Not at first. He kept going, but a little slower now. Then he felt it again and came to an abrupt stop.

It was just like he had seen on television on the few, rare occasions that he'd watched television. Sort of like slow motion.

Though no one spoke to him, the sounds blurred into one. Car horns from the street below echoed and swirled in his mind as if he could hear them perfectly and yet not hear them at all. He saw the wall about three feet away, and it seemed like it was a mile from him. He tried to lean on it, but it must have been further than he had expected.

His last thought was, "Don't close now. Please, eyes, don't close now. I can't see." His body fell to the ground in one quick motion. It was no longer slow. Once he was down, he tried to look around him but saw only darkness—something he'd been living with his entire life.

He should've felt comforted, and he did. He felt his mother's loving arms holding him tightly to her chest, a distant memory that had been long suppressed. Experts will say the human mind will never remember their first year of life, but Zach remembered now. There was no doubt about it.

The blood spilled from his stomach where the first bullet had entered. Then it poured from his back, where the second had made its passage.

There were no more voices or car horns. He could no longer feel his heart racing, full of adrenalin; full of hope. He could no longer feel. A few months shy of his sixteenth birthday, Kevin Rider, aka Zach Jacobs, boy gone missing and turned up a serial killer, had been killed.

Chapter 55

The sounds of the sirens could be heard from blocks away. The moment Alex and Amber heard them, they knew deep down in their hearts exactly what had transpired.

Alex sat on the floor of the hotel lobby, knees pulled up to her chest, and cried silently. Amber tried consoling her mother, as well as herself.

Though many in the community would pray for his death, and even dance on his grave, Amber and Alex were the only two who prayed that somehow, he had survived. That perhaps those sirens were not for him.

They had a small glimmer of hope that he was indeed alive and well and on his way to the police station. They had an even smaller glimmer of hope that he could be rehabilitated. Maybe not forgiven by the public, but forgiven by God and by himself.

Amber got up to ask the concierge where the cabstand was. They would need to go to the station to fill out a report and, more importantly, find out about Zach/Kevin. There was no easy way to find out.

They hailed a cab and headed downtown to the station. Both were exhausted. The morning had been filled with too many emotions, including the fear that Kevin was going to turn on them and add them to his long list of innocent victims.

When they arrived at the station, a police officer was already waiting for them. Alex knew immediately what happened and collapsed on the floor. Amber just turned her head and cried quietly by herself.

The officer in charge allowed them to get themselves together and then, after a few moments, offered them a seat, a beverage, and some cookies. They probably hadn't eaten or drank anything in hours, so he wanted to make sure they had something to keep their energy level up.

"What happened to my son?" Alex asked.

The officer behaved very sympathetically toward them, but it was apparent he had no real regret for what had happened to Zach. "Ms. Rider, I know you had wanted a chance for your son to get rehabilitated. We know you had the best of hopes and intentions."

"My son. What happened to him?"

"Our officers shot him. They were walking him to the squad car, and he pulled a fast one. He almost blinded Sergeant Denali, and if he'd had his way, he would've broken Officer Andrews' neck.

"He got away, running through the car garage, not caring whether or not the officers survived. It was a close call. Officer Andrews tried to just debilitate him by shooting him once, but Kevin didn't slow down. He had no choice but to shoot again.

"He's at the hospital now in the Intensive Care Unit. He's in critical condition. I have to be honest with you. The circumstances are dire. He's not expected to come out of this alive. When the ambulance reached him, he'd already been dead for over a minute. They managed to revive him and get his pulse going again, but it is slight. He lost a lot of blood. If you would prefer to go there now and see him, we can resume questioning later. I leave it up to you."

"Yes, we want to go there," Alex said without hesitation. "Now!"

"I thought so. We have a car waiting. Let's go."

They drove to the hospital at top speed with sirens blaring. Alex wasn't sure what more there was to say. Her initial meeting with her son didn't go as she had planned, and she hadn't really expected it to.

He was a serial killer and gladly admitted it to her. He didn't want a life of normalcy. Not now. It was too late. Yet, Alex still wanted to meet with him and try to get some kind of closure, some recognition of the son she held only fourteen years prior.

They were taken right to his room, and she saw him hooked up to about ten different machines monitoring his blood pressure, oxygen levels, pulse rate, etc.

He was unconscious. As she stared at him, she thought he looked like an angel. She tried not to let her heart rule her mind, but ironically, the last time she saw him alive, prior to today, he had the same angelic look.

She spoke to him in a voice barely above a whisper. It has been said that patients who are unconscious or in a coma can hear you. She figured she'd give it a try.

"Kevin, I love you and have never stopped loving you. Please know that. Not once, not a day went by that I didn't think of you, hoping that somehow and some way, you made it through OK. If there was any way I could've shielded you from the monster who stole you, I would've, and if there was any way I could've saved you, I would've given my own life."

She looked for any sign of life other than the machines pumping oxygen into his lungs. His eyes moved underneath his eyelids, but that wasn't indicative of him recognizing her; it was the body's natural function.

"Kevin, if you pull through this, and I believe that you will, please let us help you." She wrapped her arms lightly around his body and kissed his eyes. She then kissed his forehead and held his hand. She gently touched his face with her hands and kissed him once more. She knew that if he did come out of this alive, he would never let her touch him. "I love you, regardless of what you've done. Be strong."

Alex motioned for Amber to come over and speak to him. She didn't quite know what to say, so she tried to keep it light and somehow sweet. "Kevin, come on. We just got to meet each other now. It's not too late for you. We could help you."

The nurse came in and explained that visiting hours were over. She said they could come back later that evening.

Just as Alex grabbed Amber's arm to walk out, Kevin opened his eyes and managed to mumble something. They turned their heads and quickly rushed to his side. With his eyes half-opened, he whispered, "Thank you for loving me. I'm so sorry."

Alex told him again how much she loved him while trying to hold back her tears, and the nurse firmly reminded them that it was time to leave.

With great resistance, they both walked out, bowing their heads as tears dripped down their faces, and called through the open door to Kevin that they would be back. Outside of the hospital, through the double doors, the cops and hospital personnel blocked the media from entering.

As they went through the doors, they heard every rude reporter's comments. "Is he dead yet?" "Is it true he killed over ten people?" "Are his mom and sister trying to help him escape?" "Hey! There they are. A statement please?"

"No comment!" Alex said.

The police escorted them safely into the cop car, with the reporters trailing not too far behind.

"I'm sorry you had to endure that," the officer said. "That's the press. When it comes time for a good, competitive story, all traces of humanity are demolished and only the monsters come out to play. We'll try to shield you from them the best we can. Let's go to the police station and get your statement. I'm sure you must be exhausted, starving, and emotionally drained. Once we're done here, you can go back to the hospital or to your hotel room, or even back to New York. The choice is yours."

"Thank you" Alex said. "Let's just get this over with."

They gave their statements of all that had transpired in the hotel room that morning, from the second they walked in to find Kevin waiting there for them to the moment the police arrived. The officer had one thing right; they were totally exhausted. They just wanted to get this whole ordeal behind them, hope for Kevin to pull through, and take it from there.

Once the questioning had ended, but before allowing them to leave, the officer thanked them and made them aware that the fingerprints were indeed a match and that Zach and Kevin were one in the same. They also told Alex of the items found in the apartment, including the tarantula, which they had since released back into the wild.

Amber's mind shifted immediately to her dream, and she closed her eyes for a moment. It was all coming together now. Sure enough, she'd been dreaming about Kevin after all this time.

After leaving the station, Alex and Amber quickly stopped to get a bite to eat at a small restaurant in town. Afterward, they made their way back to the hospital. They wanted to be there in case there was any change, regardless of having to deal with the press.

As they walked into the ICU unit, the head nurse greeted them and asked them to sit down. She explained that Kevin had lost a lot of blood. They tried to revive him once again, but this time, they could not. Kevin Rider passed away at 4:45 p.m. He was fifteen years old.

Chapter 56

Alex couldn't give Kevin the life he deserved, but she wanted to at least give him a proper funeral. They had his body transferred to New York, where her parents, brother, other family members, and friends attended.

It was an open casket, as there was not so much as a scratch on Kevin's young face.

Some couldn't find a way to open their heart to an accused serial killer, and therefore refused to attend the funeral. But those who could look past the person he became and remember the innocent baby he once was attended and prayed for his tortured soul.

Amber had asked Tiffany to come, only promising her she would give her all of the details once everything had simmered down. She needed her best friend's support now more than ever. Tiffany was always supportive, and today wasn't any different.

Surrounding the casket were pictures of Kevin as a baby, his mother and father hugging him in a dozen different photographs. They played videos Alex had taken so many years ago, including Kevin's first steps and him kissing and hugging his twin sister. There wasn't a dry eye in the funeral home.

How was it possible that this once beautiful baby had turned into such a malicious individual? The whole situation was still so surreal.

It was a gorgeous, sunny day without a cloud in the sky. They gathered around the cemetery, and the priest gave a beautiful eulogy. They mourned for the adorable baby they once knew and, just for today, forgot the fact that this same person had caused so much pain for others. Just for today, it was Alex and Amber's day to mourn the kidnapping and killing of fourteen years ago.

Chapter 57

The day after the funeral, Amber needed to be with her best friend to mourn the loss of her brother and to reveal all of the horrific crimes he had committed. She also wanted to let her know the cause for her disturbing dreams.

Even though they saw each other at the funeral, they didn't get to talk, and Amber had so many mixed emotions; she needed to get it out.

In need of some privacy, they met at the park down the road and sat down on the bench under a shady tree. Tiffany had stopped at the ice-cream shop first and picked up a milkshake for each of them.

When they got together, Tiffany gave her best friend a long hug and they both just burst into tears. Amber was clearly upset, and Tiffany hated to see her like this. Although she was extremely curious about the details, she allowed Amber enough time to sit in silence and get her thoughts together. She would talk when she was ready.

After about twenty minutes of sitting quietly, drinking their milkshakes and listening to the birds chirping above, Amber turned toward Tiffany and was able to manage a smile. "You must be dying to know what went on."

Out of nervousness, they both started laughing and crying at the same time.

"Yes, I am, but please take your time. I can only imagine that you must be devastated, first finding out you had a twin brother and then only minutes later, finding out his whereabouts and what he was capable of."

"It was so surreal, Tiff. The whole thing started last week when I went to visit where my father used to work. I didn't really think anyone who knew my father would still be working there, but an older woman named Jill knew him and told me everything. Apparently, my mother had kept Kevin and his kidnapping from me my entire life.

"When you called that very night to show me the person on the news, I knew it was him. What are the odds of finding out that I have a brother and that he's alive, all within days of each other?

"The craziest thing is that I recognized him instantly when I turned on the news. Not only did he look like me, but he was the person who kept appearing in my dreams. It was like we had some type of weird connection, and I was able to see each and every murder he committed.

"Do you know they even found a pet tarantula in his apartment? It is such a weird feeling to know that I more or less saw such detailed portions of his life, and I hadn't seen him in fourteen years, or even knew he existed until a few days ago.

"We met with him briefly in the hotel room. It was kind of scary, not knowing if he would snap and possibly kill us too. The weird thing is that I don't think he has ever snapped. I think he always had things under control. Ironically, I still felt a bond with him. There was a strange connection of sorts, and even though he was guilty of such terrible crimes, I think he felt it too. I bet if he knew he had a family, he would've never turned to a life of murder, but under the circumstances, he was left with no other alternative.

"He suffered years of abuse at the hands of Steve, and apparently killed him when he was able. I feel like I'm supposed to hate this murderer, but he was my twin. I can't hate him. In a weird way, I love him, even though I didn't know him."

"Amber, I don't know what to say. You're such a caring and sensitive soul. It's hard to believe that anyone related to you is capable of these things. It's amazing that you were able to see his actions in your dreams. It's almost like you are psychic. This is a weird question, but does it help you any to know now why you were having those dreams?"

"I don't know if I'm psychic, as there is a lot to be said for the bond that exists between twins. You hear about it all the time in the news. As for knowing *why* I was having those dreams, it does help to know. It's also kind of scary.

"I only wish I had those dreams *prior* to him becoming a murderer, so maybe we could've tracked him down. Although I was probably too young to notice. Who knows? Maybe I did have bizarre dreams back then, but since there was no killing involved in Kevin's life, perhaps my dreams were just weird, not scary, so I didn't know any better.

"My mother showed me pictures of Kevin and me when we were younger. We looked so happy as a family and seemed to be inseparable.

"I just can't believe this is how things turned out. My heart mourns for Kevin. Though no one will miss him, other than my mother, my grandparents, my uncle, and me, I wish people would take a moment to realize the kind of life he was given and take another moment to understand. I don't expect anyone to forgive him, just recognize why he did the things he did.

"My mother is beside herself with emotion, and I don't think I can help her. She needs time to grieve by herself, so I'm staying out of her way. She sometimes blames herself for bringing Kevin outside that night, claiming him and my father might be alive if they would've gone inside five minutes earlier."

"She can't think like that, Amber. Steve could have then broken into the house and killed all of you in your sleep. Who knows? I'm just glad you are OK. I hate to sound cliché, but perhaps Kevin is in a better place now. Beneath his maliciousness, he must have had so much inner turmoil to contend with. Maybe now he's at peace, especially knowing that he did have someone who loved him all of these years."

With that, Amber started crying and just nodded her head. As she swallowed back her tears, she said, "When we were talking to him in the hotel room, I believe he did feel regret, though he wouldn't let on. It wasn't until the end, when he said he was sorry and thanked my mother for loving him. It was the most heartbreaking scene I had ever witnessed.

"Tiff, I only hope that when he died, the last thing he thought of wasn't the murders he committed but that we genuinely loved him. I hope he knew that."

Chapter 58

Alex and Amber talked a lot in the weeks that followed Kevin's death. They thought it was about time they sold the house that they had lived in after all of these years.

Amber's dreams had come full force for a few days following the events that took place, some scarier than others. Thankfully, they subsided after a few weeks and she was finally able to catch a decent night's sleep.

With all of their affairs in order and the house sold, they hired a moving company to ship their belongings. They had decided to move to a smaller house on the other side of town.

When it was time to leave, Alex reflected on the past, remembering the sweet boy that Kevin once was and mourning the young man that he would never become. There was nothing she could do now to bring back the past, and her only options were to lie down and die or move on and create a life for her and Amber. She chose the latter.

They stood together facing the house one last time, looking at the very porch where their destiny was determined and their fate was sealed that dreadful night so long ago.

As they got into the car, they shed tears for a life that was viciously stripped from them and nodded at each other to begin their new life. Promises were made to each other that from this day forward, they would begin the rest of their lives and seek happiness, though they didn't dare deny that a big part of them had died with Jack and Kevin.

While waiting to close on the new house, they stayed at Alex's parents' house. Alex's brother Keith stayed with them as well. Now that the truth was out, they came together as a family and were able to openly mourn.

For the past fourteen years, they had never stopped hoping that Kevin would one day be found, but they couldn't have imagined it would wind up like this. They all took the news of his tortured life and his demise very hard. The entire family came together for support and prayed for the soul of the boy they had lost, as well as for the victims' families, whose lives were so tragically affected.

Once Alex and Amber were ready to move into the new house, they thought of new things to do to bring them happiness, instead of reflecting on the life they'd once had. One of the things on their list was to help someone in need live a meaningful and happy life.

On an ordinary Sunday morning, they hopped in the car, plugged the address into the GPS, and made their way to the local shelter to adopt a golden retriever they saw on their website. He had one more day before he was to meet his demise. They wanted to at least be able to change *his* fate, and so that is exactly what they did. His name was Dex, and they couldn't wait to meet him.

The End

ALSO WRITTEN BY ELIZABETH PARKER:

PHOBIA

Growing up with phobias that have terrified him his entire life, Matt Brewer had finally made the decision to go to counseling, seeking help once and for all.

He entrusted his emotions in the hands of strangers and depended on them to help conquer his fear. What he did not count on was having his fears become a distinct reality, leaving him fighting for his life and the lives of those around him, including his girlfriend whom he intended to marry.

Tortured and bound, he comes face to face with evil with no one to hear his screams. Time is of the essence and it's a literal race against the clock in order to make it out alive.

*A portion of the proceeds from the sale of this book will be donated to a dog rescue organization

Finally Home

"There is a time in everyone's life where they have been emotionally inspired or amazed by something that was completely unexpected or even considered impossible. Sometimes it is so touching, that they want to share their experience with the world and tell their story.

This particular story is about a precious heart along with a free-spirited little boy who owns that heart. This little boy has expressive brown eyes, a beautiful smile, and golden brown coat that he never takes off. He also has a huge pinkish-brown nose and four very fast legs. His name is Buddy. He answers to that...when he wants to."

Buddy was a dog that no one wanted, yet he became one of the quirkiest, friendliest, smartest and most cherished of dogs. The reader is not only drawn into the book, but learns from the unfortunate mistakes of others and how to think outside of the proverbial box. It gives the reader hope that if they are going through a similar ordeal, they can also successfully overcome any related obstacle.

If you are looking for a great gift for both dog lovers and even non-dog lovers, this book is perfect. Get ready to laugh a little and perhaps even shed a few tears.

A portion of the proceeds from the sale of "Finally Home" will be donated to an animal rescue group.

Final Journey
Buddys' Book

After the publication of "Finally Home," Buddy was diagnosed with terminal cancer. Once the unthinkable happened and Buddy's precious life was cut short, his family was left heartbroken and devastated.

At the same time, in another state, poor economic conditions forced another family to give up their golden retriever.

As fate would have it, his name...was Buddy.

While they were mourning the loss of their beloved dog, another dog was mourning the loss of his treasured family.

Brought together by misfortune, they entered each other's lives to help put back together the pieces of their broken hearts.

This story is for both Buddys, producing the subtitle "Buddys' Book."

A portion of the proceeds from the sale of this book will be donated to an animal rescue organization.

Evil's Door

Childhood rumors are often prevalent in a family-oriented community. Some boast that they have seen a UFO flying overhead while others claim to have witnessed a ghost soaring through the trees. Some stories are so believable that they trickle down from sibling to sibling, friend to friend; creating a neighborhood buzz that lingers for years.

Ryan Sheffield's neighborhood was no different. Though no one would admit it, adults and children alike were freaked out by the eccentric woman who lived in the ghastly corner house, but aside from that, his world as he knew it was an ordinary one.

Bizarre situations did not surface until Ryan began working at his very first job. To his peers and superiors, it was just a traditional office. To Ryan, it was much more than that after a series of inexplicable occurrences haunted his every conscious moment.

Through a bit of intense research, he uncovered the building's gruesome history and was led down its horrifying path. He opened the door to a hell he did not want to live in and tried his best to avoid the evil that surrounded him. The truth revealed itself to him in more ways than one; a truth he was better off not knowing and one that could essentially end his life.

*A portion of the proceeds from the sale of this book will be donated to a dog rescue organization.

Made in the USA
San Bernardino, CA
19 May 2014